WISCONSIN
Public School Library Regulations
Prescribed by the State Superintendent

Name of school ‗Drummond‗‗‗‗‗‗‗‗‗‗‗‗‗‗‗

Town ‗Drummond‗‗‗‗‗‗‗ County ‗Bayfield‗‗‗
    (Village or city)

Dist. No. ‗‗one‗‗‗‗‗‗ Accession No. ‗5065‗‗‗‗
            (To be filled in by the teacher)

The librarian shall have charge of the library; keep such records and make such reports as are called for by the proper superintendent and are required by law and the library regulations of the state superintendent; and shall give out and receive books under the rules* prescribed by the state superintendent, from which the following are quoted:

RULES:

I.   The Teacher of the public school shall have charge of the Library while the school is in session and shall be responsible for the books.

II. Unless a shorter time is specified by the librarian, books may be kept two weeks without renewal.

III. Fines shall be assessed as follows:
   1. For retaining a book beyond the time limit, five cents per week, or, if so decided by the district board one cent a day.
   2. For an injury beyond ordinary wear, an amount proportionate to the injury as estimated by the Librarian.
   3. For the loss of a volume, the cost of the book.
   4. One who has incurred a fine may be refused permission to take books from the library until the fine is paid.

IV. A copy of these regulations shall be pasted upon the inside of the cover of each volume in the school district libraries, unless other approved means of marking ownership are employed.

*See "Library Regulations" in List of Books for (Township) School Libraries.

MARSHFIELD BOOK & STATIONERY, INC.

*GOAL
AHEAD!*

GOAL AHEAD!

by JOEL REEVE

S. G. PHILLIPS NEW YORK

*GOAL
AHEAD!*

1

THE ENORMOUS stadium of San Fernando University was packed in the warm November sun of California. It was a Saturday to remember, the first invasion of big-time football by the Green and White. Cheerleaders and pompon girls cavorted, foghorns bayed, colored cards flashed defiant messages at the enemy across the striped field.

Television cameras peered, wheeling and zooming in on red-capped spotters, who danced and waved their arms. The nation was watching SFU try its power and speed against the Scarlet and Gold of The University of Southern California.

Bob Westover, huge in his full padding, sat on the bench and listened to Coach Randy Randolph. Blond Bob was a giant, a pre-med junior. Star tackle, he had the legs and arms of a logger and the disposition of a St. Bernard. Next year, he would be captain of the team. Right now, he was taking a breather.

Randolph was ancient and lean. Once a great quarterback, he still possessed quick speech, strong opinions, and a bad temper.

"That Mike Caron wants it his way! Always he wants to be a star!"

"Mike is a star," Bob replied gently.

"Just because he's your roomie—" Randolph's sentence trailed off as he jumped up to shake a fist and howl at the team on the field. "Move them out! Move them! You got to move that line! Move!"

The score was USC 10, SFU 6. It was the fourth quarter and the home team had the ball on the visitor's thirty-yard line, first down and ten to go. Dan Kyle had sent Mike Caron for two precious yards to gain this position on the previous play.

Bob Westover reached for his helmet. Randolph clutched his elbow, talking a blue streak.

"We had a good season, sure. Maybe next year we can go places. Big time, Bob, big time. That's why I'm here, to put us in the big time. That's why they hired me, built this stadium. You know that. If we win this one, we make national headlines. Sure, we beat Oregon, Midwest, Stanford. That don't mean a thing. We got to get Southern Cal in order to make it. Remind Caron. And move that line, bust it open, make the running game count. Then Dan might be able to complete a pass. Use the thirty-nine series. Make them know we can run." He gaped as Dan Kyle began to call the 39. "Ohhhh . . . no!"

Kyle, a tall, square-jawed quarterback, took the

ball from center. Spinning, he faked to fullback Bill Bowers. Then he slammed the pigskin into Mike Caron's belly.

On this play Caron was to slice into the tackle slot, the guards to go straight ahead, concentrating power. All he had to do was slam and try for three or four yards.

But Mike Caron elected to move outside. Eyes flashing, he tried for the long gainer. In his mind he was crossing up not his own men but the opposition, which, he figured, was massing against SFU's push.

He forgot about Jimmy Nye, USC's defensive wizard. Nye came whirring across the scrimmage line like a rattlesnake and coiled himself around Caron's driving legs. They went down and rolled for no gain.

"Three years I've had Caron and he still hasn't learned football is a team game," Randolph groaned.

"I'll talk to him," Bob promised.

He ran onto the field, relieving big Ed Frederick, joined the huddle in time to prevent Dan Kyle from raging at Caron. "Keep with the thirty-nine series. Mike, will you follow me this time, please?"

"I know what I'm doing," Mike Caron snapped.

Kyle stared at Bob, shook his head, called the 39 left on the red, with a short count. The team wheeled and lined up with military precision and Kyle chanted numbers.

Time was running short. On the side lines a sophomore halfback named Joe Danning was staring with wide eyes, telling himself over and over that he was better than Mike Caron, better than anybody, that he should have had his chance today—and at the same time shivering for fear he would be called upon in this biggest of all games.

Coach Randolph was chewing his lip to pieces, tearing at a handkerchief in his pocket, yet trying to appear calm. Next year the schedule would be murderous unless the squad could be kept at highest pitch. If they could take this one, most of his anxiety would be relieved.

The stands were going wild in the peculiar manner of California football fans. Doctor Westover, a distinguished surgeon, was aiming his field glasses at the towering figure of his son in the white jersey with green stripes.

A couple of pretty coeds named Nancy Waite and Kathy Nelson clung to each other, unable to cheer, tense and mute in the face of crisis. They had dates with Bob Westover and Mike Caron that evening.

The band held its collective breath, hoping against hope to be able to once more play the victory march at game's end. It had been able to do so seven out of nine times this season. Victory marching was fine compensation for those who hadn't made the team.

Bob Westover assumed the stance, crouching low, measuring Bo Stone of USC, awaiting the snap back. This game had been defensively played for the most part. The opponents had scored first on a pass from Ballard to Hudgins. Then Mike Caron had run sixty yards through a broken field for a touchdown—only to have the extra point blocked. Ballard had kicked a field goal in the third quarter to take the four-point lead. Now was the home team's last chance to surge ahead.

John Foran snapped the ball back to Kyle and lunged, taking a guard with him. Bob smashed Stone to the left, lifting with his shoulder, getting a good jump, keeping contact.

Caron churned into the hole head down. He charged so quickly, middlebacker Cal Barrett of USC stumbled over Westover and Stone. Caron went for the side lines.

Again it was Jimmy Nye. He had a hound-dog's nose for the ball. Running from the right he drove into Mike with a perfect tackle.

The gain was for seven yards. It was third down and three.

"Coach wants the whole thirty-nine series. You haven't used it before," Bob reminded the huddle.

"They'll be keying on Mike," someone snapped.

"Gimme the ball. Just do some blocking, you numb-skulls up front," snarled Caron. "What's the matter with you guys? You want me to do it alone? I'll do it alone."

"You follow me, amigo," Bob cautioned.

When Kyle gave the required signal, they marched. They were bruised and battered, as most teams against USC, but they too had dished out clean, hard knocks. They were on the twenty-three, and had to make it or for another year hold their peace. Bob Westover thought, we're underdogs. But we could win. SFU was close to its highest sporting goal, a win over California's premier football team. The clock would be with SFU if the team made the first down and kept possession. Only three yards, nine feet for SFU's golden chance.

Southern Cal dug in. Jimmy Nye leaned, his bulk aimed at Kyle. The big linemen stamped their cleats into the turf. They had their own goal—the Rose Bowl. They were not about to yield without a titanic struggle.

Kyle's voice rose high and shrill, counting. He opened his hands, the ball slid into their grasp. The forward walls clashed like enemy soldiers.

Mike Caron had the ball. He was slanting off the tackle behind Bob Westover. Southern Cal sprang to meet him.

Bob turned his shoulder and knifed as Foran and Pascal, the guard, lent their bulk and strength. For a moment, it seemed possible to attain the needed distance for the first down.

Mike Caron was not in the hole. He was trying once more to fool the world and go outside. Bob made a final effort to get to the middleback, Barrett, a bull of a boy.

Jimmy Nye was there, as always, and Barrett was with him. They grabbed Mike as he got to the line of scrimmage. They held onto him and slammed him down and held him tight. Others piled on as the referee shrilled his whistle and dived among them for the ball.

The striped shirt burrowed deep enough—and discovered the pigskin lay firm in Barrett's hands.

San Fernando had lost the ball on a fumble. The golden goal faded in the shimmering late sun. Bob Westover turned and walked off the field. Beside him Mike Caron was grumbling.

"No hole, no hole! Where were you all? They stole the ball. Nye grabbed one arm, somebody else the other. They stole it!"

"That's the name of the game, amigo," Bob reminded him.

"No hole to run through! You wouldn't be linemen if you weren't dumb, but why couldn't you open it up?"

"Mike, you're a great guy and all that. But the hole was there. You just didn't run into it," Bob said sadly.

"I tell you it wasn't there!" Mike shut his mouth tight. He was a good-looking boy, with white, even teeth and a wide smile, sunny and bright on most occasions. Now he asked, "Was it there, on the level?"

They were nearing the side lines. "You'd better believe it. Randolph knows it was there," Bob said.

The coach's face was a study in anger and frustration. He stared steadily at Mike, not trusting himself to speak. Bob Westover, knowing Mike was wrong but unwilling to desert him, stood beside his friend and roommate.

"Mike, you blew it," Randolph finally said.

"I didn't see the hole. They haven't been blocking for me."

"Mike, you're a showboat, a grandstander, a hot dog! Heaven help me, in your case I can only pray for miracles."

"I tell you, the line didn't play up," Mike insisted. "I scored your only touchdown. What do you want from me?"

"If you don't learn before next season . . . it will be too bad for us both."

Bob led his friend to the bench. The defensive unit was trying to steal back the ball, but the recovered fumble had bolstered USC's determination. Hudgins was running behind good blocking for short yardage. He coolly crossed up SFU by throwing a down-and-in pass to his end, who took the ball past midfield.

A gun went off and with it SFU's last forlorn hope of victory. The sun seemed to darken although the sky was cloudless. The Green-and-White squad trotted miserably toward the glittering dressing rooms of their brand new field house beneath the stadium.

Bob and Mike had adjoining lockers. In the sullen silence of defeat they did not exchange words until they had showered and were dressing.

Mike began, "Look, I didn't mean you. I know you're in there every minute."

"The hole was there for you, amigo." Bob refused to let the halfback off the hook.

"Maybe it was. I thought I could outrun them. I thought they wouldn't be expecting it again so soon." Mike paused, lowered his voice. "You know I need those headlines."

"Bad thinking, amigo," Bob told him.

"I have to think that way. Don't forget, I'm here on a scholarship. I want to spend a few years as a pro, making money. I have to scratch. Why do you think I play this fool game?"

"Most of us play because we love it." Bob shook his head, pausing as he knotted his tie. "No, wait a minute, Mike. I know how it is with you. I know you feel you have to be a star and I understand why. But you're going about it wrong, amigo, really wrong."

Mike shrugged. "Football's the only chance I've got. You don't have to be a star. You shouldn't even be on the squad, risking your hands. You could ruin your whole medical career out there."

"Let's not worry about me. Like you say, my future is assured." There was a bit of irony in Bob's voice. "Now hurry and finish dressing. We've got to take the girls to The Grove, remember? For the great victory party. Some party!"

They walked past the other men, who already were beginning to throw off the sadness of defeat. There would be another year. They had not, after all, been expected to do nearly as well. Their season had been a magnificent success until the fourth quarter of today's game.

The door to Randolph's office was closed. Bob and Mike hesitated, then decided not to attempt to speak with the head coach. They left the field house and walked across the campus toward the junior dormitory, a low-slung building surrounded by lush California planting.

People thought the students a strange duo. Bob was the wealthy son of a widowed surgeon, Mike the grandson of Italian immigrants, an orphan without money who had fought his way to the university with sheer courage. The two had been friends since high school. Their oppositeness had brought them together, Bob reflected. Mike's fire balanced Bob's calm.

The giant blond youth and the smaller dark one were silent, each with his own thoughts, as they entered the junior dorm.

2

THE BOYS' ROOM in the junior dorm was modern, bright, and well furnished. It was air-conditioned, centrally heated and ventilated. It contained two built-in table-desks. Day beds, in plaid, made couches across the room from each other. There were ample, well-filled bookshelves and two typewriters—one a portable electric and the other a manual. SFU pennants and award plaques given to the occupants for services rendered adorned the walls. Hanging there also were a Braque print and a Pop Art rendition of a can of beans.

The windows overlooked the campus, a vista which spread to the athletic fields and encompassed fabulous buildings housing classrooms and laboratories. SFU considered itself the heaven of the collegiate world, where all the latest and best was provided for the largest number of students congregated in one place.

Bob Westover had contributed to the room a color television set complete with UHF for educational programs and a portable radio-record player with dozens of stereo records.

Necessities included an adjacent bathroom and two large closets, a pair of ample bureaus, and comfortable easy chairs, whose legs dug into the wall-to-wall carpeting.

Mike Caron's first act, upon returning to the room, was to take a look at his bank book.

The initial deposit, accumulated by hard work, had been $3,800. Thereafter no deposits were listed. Withdrawals ran their monotonous course down to $118.00.

Mike shut the book grimly and dropped it back into the drawer. At least, he comforted himself, he was paid up for the rest of the year. He had slightly more than one hundred dollars to play with until summer vacation, unless he could wangle a part-time job now that the football season was over. He took a small wad of bills, a fiver and fifteen singles, and slid them into another trophy of the pigskin wars—a money clip of gold. He opened the bottom drawer and removed a white shirt, black tie, shorts, and black socks.

From his closet he took a tuxedo jacket and the striped trousers to match. He unwrapped his hardly used calfskin shoes from tissue.

Bob was dressing rapidly. Unthinkingly he said, "That jacket's wrong . . . Why don't you wear my navy blue tonight? I can see my reflection in yours."

"Please, Ma, I'd rather wear my own."

"Okay . . . Okay." Bob frowned. His roomie was

becoming more and more sensitive. "I'm sorry, I'm sorry."

Mike said, "Forget it. I'm the grouch. The day's been pretty bad, hasn't it?"

"It hasn't been a sweet success," Bob agreed. "Tonight, though, we'll relax and forget our problems."

Mike started to dress. His nerves were raw, he realized. Too many things were plaguing him. His mistakes in the big game were becoming clear. He dimly recognized that he was pushing too hard in too many directions.

However, that was the only way he knew how to live. Poor from birth, orphaned in high school, he had had to make his own way, every hard step. Nevertheless he had accepted only what he felt he had earned, no more. Overproud and oversensitive was Mike Caron, but nothing could be done about it.

Bob Westover had been a helpful friend and a leavening influence up until now. Mike had let Bob pay more than his share, since Bob had money to burn and didn't downgrade Mike. Lately, though, Bob's affluence had irked Mike. He could hardly wait for the day when he'd be able to repay Bob.

Mike's moods puzzled Bob Westover. The blond giant was something of a sentimentalist. He had a dogged, deep belief in the responsibilities and benefits of friendship. He was aware of Mike's financial problem and felt it no betrayal to sneak occasional glances at the diminishing bank-book figures. Any aid that

19

could be given Mike without shattering the Caron pride—since Doctor Westover was a wealthy man and Bob was an only child—was legitimate in Bob's lexicon.

Mike's resentment was becoming apparent. Their disagreement on the field today was only an extension of the problem. Bob, telling Mike he'd meet him downstairs, mulled over the situation on his way to the campus parking lot. He tickled his Mustang two-by-two into life, picked up Mike at the dorm's front door, and gave his roomie a friendly grin. Two friends could work out anything. They tooled over to the coed row of dorms and blew a distinctive "my-dog-has-fleas" horn, Mike's contribution to the partnership in the car, and the two girls came tripping across the mall.

Nancy was dark, Kathy blonde. Fate had arranged the color contrast. Nancy Waite was Bob's girl, Kathy Nelson, Mike's. Both coeds were nineteen, pretty, and came from well-to-do families. Both studied in the Economics School and made the first third in grades with ease. Because they were gay and genial companions to the two athletes, Nancy and Kathy were the envy of their sorority house.

The foursome was bound for The Grove, a supper club that featured swing bands and star entertainers. College kids and young marrieds willingly paid stiff prices to have fun there. The Grove, the only establishment of its kind in the entire valley, was stylish. Tonight SFU was to have celebrated at a victory dinner ... Not to show up and congratulate the Southern Cal men who would be present for that very purpose, would have been cowardly.

"What happened today was bad luck. Just bad luck," Nancy clucked.

"I thought you had 'em," Kathy said to Mike. "There in the last few minutes, I thought so."

"We almost did at that," Bob agreed. "The opposition was very good. That Jimmy Nye, he's a tiger."

"Jimmy Nye is a fink," said Mike harshly. "A great defensive back, but a fink."

"He's been bugging you for a long time, hasn't he?" Nancy asked innocently.

"I've beaten him to a nubbin, in track, in football, baseball, everything. Until today," Mike added. "He really got even today."

"That's right. Mike always beat Jimmy, even in grade school," remembered Bob. He had to force himself not to mention that Mike could have whipped Nye again this afternoon if Mike had followed Bob's blocking. He was determined to bring off this evening without a clash.

"Some guys," said Mike, "you play against them time after time and you get to like them. Jimmy is different. He's like an enemy."

"He's quick with his mouth," Bob said. "But he's all right, really. I know his people, they live near us."

"Him and his millionaire father." Mike's dark face glowered. "He's spoiled rotten."

"Oh, come on, Mike, he's kind of cute," said Kathy. "Not my type, but fun and stuff."

"He's no fun in my book." Mike relapsed, sulking. Nothing this day had gone right; nothing would, he thought.

They parked at the rear of The Grove and found their way into the club. The band was playing, the room filled with college men and their dates. Huge banners of green and white and scarlet and gold were in evidence. The four were escorted by a brown-jacketed maitre d' to a reserved table near the dance floor. Hudgins and Ballard, good and worthy adversaries, waved greetings. Bob swallowed when he observed how closely seated to them were Jimmy Nye and his current flame, Bobo Hill. Before they could order Jimmy Nye loomed behind Bob, grinning across at Mike. He was about Mike's size and build. Nye wore his mouse-brown hair long and combed across his forehead, so that a lock made a parenthesis on that side of his narrow, hatchetlike face. His green eyes were full of mockery.

"Well, old Mike, old slob, got you today, didn't we?"

"You did, indeed." Mike tried to keep it light.

"Took many a long year," Jimmy confessed, addressing any and all. "But today old Mike couldn't find his holes and Jimmy was on the job. It sure felt good, old Mike."

"You did it well," Mike told him. He was finding it more and more difficult to maintain a weak smile.

Bob broke in, trying to ease the moment. "You had

some help, Jimmy. Your guys were mighty tough in there."

The USC back waved a hand. "We're always tough. Watch us in the Bowl game."

Mike asked, "You planning to beat Ohio State?"

"Murder'em. Pure murder." Jimmy switched his attention to Kathy. "Missy, how about it?"

"How about what?" asked the blonde girl.

"A dance. To the victor belongs the spoils. We won, I claim the first dance." He reached out a hand to her.

Kathy, startled, looked at Mike. Trying to keep calm, he shrugged. Kathy arose and Jimmy swept her into his arms, speaking for once in a lowered voice.

"You have to hand it to him for gall," Bob commented.

"Jimmy is cute," Nancy chirped. "Nervy, but cute. There's something about him I like."

Mike analyzed that something. The sons and daughters of wealth had an air about them. They were easy, confident, assured. Bob Westover, too, was that way. Mike had tried hard to copy, but couldn't quite pull it off.

Nancy was prattling, "Jimmy used to be crazy about Kathy, you know."

That remark dampened the evening. The waiter finally produced the bill and Bob reached for it. Mike took out his money clip.

"Let this one be on me," Bob offered.

"Let it be Dutch, as always." Mike's tone was sharp.

Bob hesitated, then shrugged. "Have it your way. How about a four-dollar tip?"

Mike set down his packet of bills. "Make it six. The waiter has to slog it out for his dough."

Bob added his share, noting Mike's empty money clip before it was shuffled back into his pocket. The boys, silent, followed the chattering girls to the parking lot. It was a balmy evening, but the boys just couldn't take pleasure in it. They got into the car. Bob pointed it toward the college.

As they came to the wide main road, a two-seater Porsche slid alongside them. Jimmy Nye was driving, one arm around flame-tressed Bobo.

"Still driving that Detroit iron?" gibed the USC man.

"No class at all, Jimmy," agreed Bob amiably.

They drove neck and neck for a hundred yards. Then Jimmy said, "Well, so long, slow freight," and kicked at the accelerator. The Porsche shot ahead.

"Get him, Bob," urged an angry Mike. "Show him."

Instinctively Bob stepped on the gas. The Mustang's speedometer rose steadily. Bob shifted through the gears. He was proud of the little car's ability. The Mustang gradually crept behind the foreign job.

Jimmy, eye on the rear-vision mirror, promptly maneuvered to prevent Bob from passing him. It was a juvenile move, and dangerous.

"Get him!" yelled Mike. "Push him off the road." Instantly, as if hearing him, the driver of the Porsche slowed. Jimmy drew her to the side of the road, allowing Bob to come abreast, then leaped from the car as Bob braked and emerged. Bob's face was hot and angry. So was Jimmy's.

"I heard what Mike said. I call that dirty pool."

Mike was out of the Mustang in a flash. "What do you call what you were doing?"

Jimmy did not stand upon ceremony. Before Bob could stop him he swung, aiming for Mike's head.

Mike felt good for the first time since the fourth quarter of the football game. He let Jimmy's punch slide by. Mike had earned a lot of his money at hard labor, among men who fought as often as they ate dinner. He brought up a solid left to the body.

Jimmy floundered back. He danced a moment, trying to organize an attack. Mike stalked him, jabbing, crossing, intent on destruction. He bloodied Jimmy's eye, then hooked to the chin. He was moving in to hammer Jimmy hard when he was caught from behind, lifted, and held powerless by Bob Westover.

"Let me go," Mike raged. "I'll take him apart!"

"You could, at that. But should you?" Bob was calm even as he held Mike in a vise. "You know you can do it and so does he, now."

Mike's vision cleared. He saw a pale, forlorn Jimmy leaning against the Porsche, blood streaming from his eye and nose, defenseless, somehow terribly pitiable. The girls were silent, watching Bobo wipe at the gore.

Mike relaxed and Bob turned him loose. There was a moment of uncertainty. Then Mike swallowed hard and took a tentative step toward Jimmy.

25

"Hey, I'm sorry. I didn't mean to. . . ."

Bobo glared at him. "You meant to kill him," she said flatly. "That's the way you are, your kind. Just get going, bub, just leave us alone."

Bob tugged gently at Mike's sleeve. "Let's go."

In the car the silence continued. They had arrived at the girl's dorm before Kathy broke it.

"Jimmy started it," she said. "Maybe you shouldn't have beat him so badly, Mike. But he started it and you couldn't very well have done anything else."

"Thanks," said Mike drily.

"Kathy's right," Nancy agreed. "It's too bad it had to happen. But Jimmy asked for it."

"Yeah, well," said Mike. "Good night, Kathy . . . Nancy."

Bob turned the car about. At the dorm he parked and they walked to their room. They hung up their clothing and unmade the beds and got into them. Neither was at all sleepy.

"Forget what happened tonight, Mike. You did what you had to do," Bob said.

"I'd have really hurt Nye if you hadn't stopped me."

"I know. It's because you've got things on your mind, amigo. You really weren't yourself tonight." Bob was carefully casual. "You're worried about money."

"I can handle it," Mike snapped, too quickly.

"The scholarship isn't enough and you know it and I know it. Look, why don't you let me go to my father and make a straight, business loan? You can pay it back when you graduate. What's wrong with that?"

Mike turned to face his roommate across the space between the beds. "I don't borrow. My father didn't borrow, poor as he was. His father borrowed to get to this country and spent his life repaying. I can't borrow. I never will."

"The entire world runs on credit, but not Mike Caron," Bob said, sighing.

"And look at the world!"

"Mike, you can't go through school and not relax, have some fun. What will you do now—wait tables? You need some extras, we all do."

"You've picked up enough tabs for me."

"I'd pick up more. Can't have you spoiling our fun . . . Nancy's and Kathy's and mine, too."

"Kathy understands."

"Sure, but why go through it all? We only attend college once. Let's enjoy it."

Mike said, suddenly gentle, "You're a great guy, Bob. I do appreciate what you're suggesting. But I've only got one big thing, my independence. Keeping that's a religion with me, I guess. I can't owe money."

There was nothing more to be said. Bob grunted, snapped off the light. "Okay, stubborn."

"So I'm stubborn."

They could sleep now that the financial problem was in the open. Neither boy could have endured ending the night with so much unsaid between them.

3

CHRISTMAS IN THE southern part of California is enthusiastically observed, as everywhere, but those accustomed to snow find sun and warmth incongruous. Santa Claus parades down Hollywood Boulevard nightly, in full regalia, but there are no sleighs in evidence. Bob Westover had spent several holidays in New York before his mother's death and realized Mike Caron's predicament. He dialed Mike Caron at the dormitory.

"Hello, Mike?"

"Hiya, Bob?"

"How about a picnic? Can't guarantee any snow but we could drive up to Big Elk. There'll be some Peekays around but we can duck them. The girls are eager."

"Sounds all right." Mike was restless and unhappier than he chose to admit. "When?"

"Tomorrow morning, about eight?"

"Okay."

Bob said good-bye and hung up. He had exchanged gifts with his father earlier, before the famed surgeon had had to make a call at the hospital. Mike was without family, Bob scarcely saw what remained of his. My roomie and I have a lot in common, all right, Bob reflected.

But Mike was penniless, something Bob had never had to contend with. Money made a huge difference. San Fernando University was basically democratic. No real snobbery marred the school. But the Peekays—short for Phi Kappas—were a rich bunch and many of the football players belonged to that fraternity. Bob had chosen not to join a club and Mike had gone along with him, although there were advantages to belonging. The Peekays owned a private camp on Big Elk, to the east of the college.

Bob tooled the Mustang over to Nancy's house. He could spend Christmas day with the Waite family. Mike was not so fortunate. The Nelson family drove north to San Francisco each year. Kathy would fly back for the picnic tomorrow but could not avoid the clan dinner.

Something had to be done about Mike, Bob knew. His athletic scholarship took care only of tuition and books. Meals could be had in Commons for little money. SFU did not pamper its athletes, although it did allow graduate organizations to advance small sums in cases of need. Mike Caron pigheadedly did not allow anyone to loan him money.

He had failed to bag a part-time holiday job in the

post office and was shorter of temper than before. Mike was becoming hard to live with these days, Bob admitted.

Yet Bob felt responsibility. He really wanted to help.

At Nancy's, Bob was drawn into defense of Mike when Bobo dropped in to exchange gifts.

"Mike is a beast," Bobo declared. "What you kids see in him is more than I can imagine."

"Mike's got problems," Nancy offered.

"Bobo doesn't appreciate SFU," Bob scoffed. "She goes with USC men."

"Jimmy Nye is worth ten of Mike," stated Bobo, her voice rising. "He's a fun person. Mike causes trouble, always."

"You have fun," Bob advised her. "We'll stick with Mike."

"You're stuck with him, you mean." Bobo laughed unpleasantly and departed, not in the spirit of Christmas.

"She's a pain in the elbow," Bob said to Nancy.

"I know. But what *are* we going to do about Mike? Kathy is so worried, she's losing weight. Her family is thinking about taking her out of the dorm and making her commute from Westwood. They claim it's our diet."

"Big deal, driving over the freeway from Westwood." But the fact the discussion had arisen at all was disturbing.

Bob pondered the situation off and on until time to

pick up Mike and the girls the following morning. He hoped a holiday spent at school with other orphans or misplaced students had not completely embittered Mike. Bob honked the tricky horn and watched Mike stride across the walk to the car. "Hey, you're on time."

Mike's heavy blue sweater was thrown into the back seat of the car. "Happy day after Christmas. What did Sandy Claws bring you, big man?"

Bob pointed to his left wrist, bedecked with a self-winding sports watch. "And a check, which I intend spending on the four of us this week of leisure."

"Nice going." Mike admired the timepiece. "Got a small gift myself."

Bob was surprised that Mike had not swiftly resented his proposal to take care of expenses for the holiday week. "Like what?" They had silently agreed, because of Mike's lack of cash, not to exchange presents this Yuletide.

"Like a week-end job in the dining room. You know that Cashman fellow, the tall track man? He dropped out. The dean gave me the job."

"That's wonderful," Bob congratulated warmly. "The job will take care of all your little expenses. Now, if you'll let Dad loan you. . . ."

"Loan me no loans." Mike's laugh was not bitter. "I'll get by as long as I can wait tables. Now let's get going to the cold country in them thar hills."

The girls, still bubbling with Christmas spirit, were at the dorm, waiting. Mike stowed the baskets of food they had prepared in the rear deck and Bob turned the blunt nose of the car eastward. They drove off in a barrage of loud talk and laughter.

The freeways were uncrowded and the road to the mountains presented little difficulty. By noon they were overlooking a deep, steep gorge. Big Elk, only fifty miles from the school, was more than seven thousand feet high. Usually at this time of year skiers swarmed down the slopes, but the sun this season had proven too much for the occasional snows. The peaks across the valley were snow-capped, all was lush and serene. The foursome unloaded, spread blankets, turned on the transistor radio, and lounged. This break in the academic year was as welcome to them as it is to students the world over.

They talked.

Mike said dreamily, "This summer I'll muscle up, put on some weight, and maybe go out for fullback. I've got to make the pro's. I'll need the money."

Bob said, "That sounds easy to me. I'll be slaving away over nasty diseases."

"Think of us, dedicated to hot stoves," murmured Kathy.

"The better to feed us, my dears."

"Which reminds me, when do we eat?"

They opened the baskets and removed cold turkey, ham and pickles on thin-sliced bread, soft drinks in a special cooler, and slabs of pumpkin pie, whose crust was a bit soggy, as everyone informed Kathy promptly.

"I'm only a sophomore. I'll learn," the girl defended herself.

"Imagine trying to learn to cook in college. What ever happened to girls who were taught by their mothers? Housewives in frilly aprons?"

"Everything's different," Bob told Mike. "Today, it's cans."

They felt lazy, and leaned back against tree trunks, and surveyed the wonders of nature. From down the road toward the lake they planned to visit later came the sounds of voices raised on high. Jimmy Nye would be at the Peekay camp on the lake with his fraternity brothers. USC also had a chapter. Perhaps it would not be a good idea, Bob mused, to visit that section of the Big Elk country this afternoon.

The more he thought about it, the more he disliked the notion of being within hearing distance of the acid-tongued footballer from USC. Mike was in good spirits; it would be a shame to spoil his day. Bob rose and walked close to the edge of the cliff and looked down into the green valley below.

"Come look! Imagine flowers blooming in December! There are actually wildflowers down yonder." The pink and white flowers covered not only the valley bottom but the slope leading to it.

The other three joined him. "I'd like to get down there and sniff around," Mike said.

"Oh, fine! And how would you get back up here?"

"Makes me dizzy just to think about it." Nancy drew back.

"I'm dizzy enough as it is," said Kathy. "How about visiting the Peekays? They have boats on the lake."

33

Bob said quickly, "It is beautiful down in the valley." He leaned forward, putting his left hand on a protruding rock. "Oh, no!" he cried.

The stiff, new band of his Christmas watch had opened and the expensive timepiece was falling, falling. It landed on the slope near a patch of pink flowers. They kept staring, holding their breath, as people do when watching tumbling objects.

"My father will be furious," Bob was muttering. "The one thing he can't stand is carelessness."

"Not your fault," said Mike. "He should give you presents with good, solid clasps."

"It's a shame, that lovely watch," Nancy commented. "I wonder if it's damaged? Oh, do you think it can be rescued?"

"Forget it," Mike advised them. "Or get a rope."

"The Peekays!" Kathy remembered. "They'll have ropes!"

Bob swung over the edge. "I was climbing the Alps when you were all in diapers," he told them. "You may tell the world I performed this heroic feat for loss of a watch."

"You fool, come back!"

Bob slid down a few yards, grinned up at them. "You see? I'm a mountain goat."

"The tops of those pines down there are like stakes. Sharp stakes. If you fall you'll be killed."

"Ha! Fear not," called Bob. He was making good progress, hand over hand, finding roots and projecting rocks to aid him. It was true that as a boy he had spent a summer in Switzerland and had occasionally climbed up and down cliffs. Now he felt strong and confident.

"But how do you get back?" Mike asked.

Bob paused and laughed. "You think I forgot about that small detail? In the back of the car, amigo, there is a tow line. A fine, special, long one. Okay?"

He took hold of a small, thick bush. He reached down toward the shining watch near the wildflowers. He had to stretch. He nipped the watch between his fingers, shook it merrily at those above, tucked it into his pocket. "You see?"

Then the little bush gave way. Mike let out a shout of dismay. Bob grabbed, found no handgrip. Stones rolled beneath him as he slid, gaining momentum. Time seemed to stand still for those who watched. Would he hurtle down into the treetops?

Suddenly Bob found his balance. He grabbed at roots and aimed for a ledge. It was his one hope. He struck the rocky floor of the narrow ledge with tremendous force. He lay there, sprawled, his consciousness running away like water down a drain. . . .

Mike took command, managed to keep his voice calm as he spoke to the terror-stricken girls.

"Nancy, open the deck of the car. Get the rope. . . . Kathy, you can run. Get down to the Peekay camp and bring more rope and everybody who can hold onto an end of it. Someone'll drive you back here. Hurry!"

Kathy had won a few girls' track events in the past.

She took off like a gazelle, running toward the lake. Nancy did not move. She stood staring down at the still figure of Bob Westover.

"Supposing . . . supposing he rolls over?" she whispered.

"He won't while he's knocked out. People don't. Will you get the rope?" Mike had also thought about the possibility of the big body spinning off the small ledge. He dared not attempt to get down there without the rope. He'd just seen the danger of that move. Mike tried to think. Nancy recovered herself and ran to the car, opened the rear deck, and returned with the thin but strong tow line. "Here."

She took Mike's place, watching for signs of returning consciousness in Bob. Mike went to the nearest tree and made a bight, then carried the end of the rope to cliff's edge. Unfortunately the rope was pitifully short. He took a deep breath and resumed his vigil beside Nancy.

She moaned, "I'm scared, Mike."

"It'll be all right." Would it? He wasn't at all sure.

"Supposing they don't have enough rope to reach him?"

"In the bunch of them? There'll be plenty of rope."

"But if he's badly hurt?"

"I'll bring him up, I tell you."

"Oh, Mike, I'm so scared."

They stayed there even when they heard the automobiles approaching, even when Kathy appeared at their side, even when Jimmy Nye came with more tow lines and began tying them together, not speaking to Mike, but working with deft sure hands, taking charge, ordering others about.

When the line was ready, however, Mike got up and gently but firmly took the coil from Jimmy. Six of the Peekays, including Ballard and Stone from the football team, stood by, ready to help in any way.

Another car drew up, men came running. One, a sharp-eyed fellow in his late twenties, carried a motion-picture camera. "I'm from the *Star-Times*," he announced. "Is that really Bob Westover down there?"

"It's not Mickey Mouse," snapped Jimmy Nye.

The photographer ignored him, stared at Mike. "And you're Caron, his roomie. You going to climb down there?"

"No, he's going to take off and fly," sniped Nye. "Keep out of the way, Kitzinger." He explained to the others, "This is Joe Scoop, the demon reporter. A real gasser."

"Forget Joe," said Mike impatiently. "Just watch that line, will you?"

He swung over the ledge and step by step began to make his cautious way down the slope. Once he scraped himself badly and had to stop. Once, he dangled dangerously while the others gasped, then regained a foothold. When he reached the ledge he tied the rope around his waist.

Bob opened his eyes as Mike leaned close. "Got . . . the wind . . . knocked out of me, I guess."

"Got a knock on the head," Mike said. "Don't move.

37

Just let me make sure nothing's broken. I can hold you here until they get a bosun's chair or something."

"I'm kind of numb. Pinched a nerve, maybe."

"Don't move," Mike begged him. He looked up. Joe Kitzinger's camera was trained on them. "Joe, send somebody for the forest-ranger crew."

Jimmy Nye's face came into view. "Is Bob hurt bad? What can we do?"

"Hi, Jimmy Nye. I'll be all right." Bob gingerly stirred, managed to sit up.

"You're not moving your legs," Mike noted sharply.

"They're numb, all right." Now Bob was scared. "Maybe I'm not all right. I guess we'd better wait for help."

"Kathy, send down my sweater with the rangers." Mike turned back to Bob. "Lie down. They've trained rangers to handle situations like this. We only need to stay quiet."

"Not much else I can do." Bob was sweating despite the cool air of the mountains. "If it's just a nerve. . . ."

"You're not a doctor yet," reminded Mike. "Don't diagnose." He made sure Bob could not roll toward the ledge's edge.

"Too bad I had to be a mountain goat," Bob groaned.

"So what else is new?"

From above could be heard the screech of tires and the girls' excited voices. "The rangers! They're down there. Oh, help them!"

"That's what we're here for, girlie."

Full-brimmed hats appeared. Eyes focused on the ledge. By rope the rangers slid a basket-stretcher down the side of the cliff, came scrambling after it, sustained by their own lines.

"Nice thinkin', Caron. Help us ease your pal onto this, huh?" one of the men asked.

It was not as easy as it sounded. Bob's legs were heavy and inanimate. It took them some time to get him properly strapped in. Then the winch above began to operate. The rangers steadied the basket as they climbed with it. Mike, shivering, was left alone on the ledge.

"Hold tight, Caron. They'll pull you up in a few minutes," Kitzinger called.

Mike started thinking. This story would be good for a lot of press mileage. He and Bob were well known. The newspapers would carry pictures and a feature article. Caron attempts rescue. Not bad publicity. He made up his mind. "Never mind. I got down here, I can make it back."

"Don't," Kitzinger warned.

Mike began climbing up the rope, hand over hand, aware only of the camera. This would make a good shot for the paper, he thought.

"Hey, that's fine. You're doing all right. Kick out a little once, will you? I need a wider angle."

Mike shoved his foot against the wall, pushed himself away from the slope.

"One more time," pleaded Kitzinger.

Mike kicked harder this time, then realized immediately that he was out of control. He spun halfway around, crashed against the cliff with terrific force. His hip struck a sharp rock. The pain was instant and intense. He thought he would faint and held onto the rope by sheer instinct. The gorge yawned below.

Summoning all his reserves, grinning into the camera's eye, Mike began to climb again. He reached the top with Kitzinger still grinding away. "Hurt yourself, Caron?" The newspaperman's sharp eyes glinted.

"No, not really." Mike wiped the pain from his face. No one must know about his injury. "I'm okay. Shouldn't you be getting shots of Bob?"

Kitzinger reacted, filming Nancy's expression as she watched the rangers tenderly probe Westover's legs. Mike managed to approach the Mustang without limping. Kathy helped him into the car.

"Your leg, you did hurt it."

"Yes," he said. "But not badly. Don't breathe a word, you hear? Not now, not any time. C'mon, we'll follow Bob down to the hospital."

"That won't be necessary. Look."

"Ouch! Hey, it was a pinched nerve," Bob was yelling. He stood up, took a few tentative steps, then said with confidence, "Hey, I'm all right! Hey, thanks everybody. I was a real dope to go mountain goating. Jimmy, all of you, I apologize."

"Glad you're okay. Forget it and come on down to the lake."

40

"No, we've had it for today," Mike announced from the car. "Come on, Bob, let's go home."

"Mike doesn't want to play," Jimmy Nye sneered.

"That's right," said Mike. "It hasn't been fun. Are you coming, Bob?" Pain was playing a tune up and down Mike's right leg. The publicity wouldn't be worth it, he regretted. Nothing was worth it.

4

KITZINGER DID NOT fail to make the most of his story and his film. The episode was shown on local television during the day. The morning papers also carried it, but the *Star-Times* had the most definitive article.

"Bob Westover, son of a wealthy Bel-Air physician was saved from death yesterday by his companion, SFU football teammate, Mike Caron. The two boys were mountain climbing with two socially prominent coeds, Miss Kathy. . . ."

"Enough, enough!" cried Mike as Bob unctuously mimicked the newscaster.

"Mike Caron, hero of the episode, is expected to make All America under SFU Coach Randy Randolph next season," continued Bob. He peered at Mike. "Some build-up! I salute you, Mr. All."

"Knock it off." Mike was thoughtful, easing his leg

as he lay on his bed. "The build-up doesn't hurt any, you know."

"All ink is good ink, is that it?"

"No, no." Mike's forehead creased. "Maybe you're bugged because the newscaster didn't say you're All-American material."

"Don't be silly."

Mike grinned at him. "Do you ever read any of your clippings?"

"Sure." Bob threw the paper into the wastebasket. "How's that leg?"

"Pain comes and it goes. How's yours?"

"Just a bit sore. Dad says it won't bother me. I wish you'd let him examine you."

"I'm all right." Mike was not all right. His right leg was acting independent of his wishes. At times it obeyed. Then it would buckle. The peculiar injury would, he thought, vanish entirely if he ignored it. He thought Bob had suffered a worse jolt.

"Well, lots of luck." Bob started for the door, paused. "Sure you don't want to go to the party?"

"I'm sure. Not without Kathy. She's doing something with the Junior League tonight—you know, socially prominent stuff."

"Well, I'll be seeing you." Bob was staying at home for the holidays but could not refrain from visiting the campus each day.

When the door closed Mike got up and walked the length of the room. He felt no pain. Vastly relieved, he swung around and an arrow shot into his hip. He clenched his teeth until the pain went away. He walked again. As long as he did not pivot the leg seemed to work all right.

Someone knocked. Mike sat down hastily in an easy chair and seized a textbook. "Come in," he called.

The big young man who opened the door was red-haired and green eyed. His nose was too large for his face and had been broken and reset. He was Joe Danning, the sophomore who had for the past season acted as Mike's replacement, and who believed he was just as good, if not better, than any halfback in the country.

"You okay, Mike?"

"Come on in, sit down," Mike said, wishing the boy would go away. "Why shouldn't I be all right?"

"Well, I saw what happened on the box. Looked like you got banged up a little."

"Nothing to it. Just one of those things. Kitzinger happened to be over at the Peekay camp with his lousy camera." Mike was explaining too much, he realized. He changed the subject. "How are you getting along in classes, Joe?"

"Rough," admitted the redhead, seating himself gingerly in Bob's chair. "Math is really something. I never was any good at math."

"What's your major?"

"I started with Business Engineering. But it didn't work out. I'm Phys. Ed."

That was the course all the nonintellectual students

finally studied, Mike knew. Danning was attending SFU on a football scholarship. He had been a prep-school star somewhere in the Middle West.

"You'll do all right . . . if you don't mind studying."

"I don't mind. I'm just not very good at it." Danning sighed, looking around. "Nice place you guys have here."

"We like it."

"What do you think about USC and Ohio State in the Bowl?"

Mike shrugged. "Ohio State will plaster 'em. We should have beaten them."

"Yeah." Danning was silent a moment, then added, "You were great on that long run. That's my style. It makes a guy feel good, running on his own, ducking 'em, givin' them the arm. I've got a bad break here, you know."

"You don't like it here?"

"I don't play. You do."

"Oh, I see." Mike understood what Joe meant.

"There's only a year between us. By the time I get to play regular, you're already in the pro's. I get one year to star."

"You'll play more often next season."

"But you're number one."

"That's tough for you." Danning's attitude annoyed Mike. He made a suggestion. "You could lay off a year and enter another college."

Danning shook his head. "My grades aren't good

enough. I'm a year behind now. They held me in prep school. I almost didn't get in here. You see, my folks are poor."

"Mine are dead," Mike said shortly.

"Oh, I didn't know." Danning gestured awkwardly. "This room, everything. . . ."

"I'm just lucky. Bob Westover furnished this place. He's rich. I work for my spending money."

"Sure. I work too, during vacations." Danning relaxed. "Hey, we're a lot alike, aren't we?"

"Are we?" Mike was cold to the idea.

"Sure. No money. Scholarship guys. Halfbacks . . . runnin' backs, both of us. We want to make the pro's."

"How do you know I want to play professional ball?"

"Can't miss. You've got all the moves, you need the money. And you block. Pro backs have to block, but how many college runnin' backs can block?"

"Not many."

"I'm for the pro's, too. When I'm washed up there I'll coach." Danning's jaw muscles worked. "You know how it is. When a guy is on his own he thinks about the future."

"That's right. He better had," Mike admitted.

"You do," Danning declared.

"Do I?"

"Sure. Secretly, you're worried. About money, about your future, even about me. It's too bad we're on the same team." Danning rose to go. "I'll be trying to beat you out."

"That's the name of the game."

"You know what? I was really hoping you were hurt yesterday. That's rotten, I have to admit. But when a guy wants something bad enough, I guess he just don't care about anyone else." Danning shook his head. "I apologize for that, thinking that way. I know it's wrong. On the other hand, you can't blame me, can you?"

"No, I can't blame you," Mike assured him.

"Well . . . see you at the Rose Bowl. Thanks for talking to me." Danning was not so poised for a moment. "I don't have a friend like Westover. I don't make friends easy."

"Come around any time," said Mike, not meaning it.

"Thanks . . . thanks. But Westover wouldn't care for that." Danning nodded and left the room.

The tough redhead was right. Bob Westover would not care to have anything to do with him. Bob was no snob. He just had good taste. Danning was too blunt.

Too honest?

Mike squirmed, got up, tried again to pivot on his right leg. It hurt. He fought down fear. After all, he had been clobbered a hundred times on the field. He had been hurt just as painfully and had returned to the game after a brief rest. He was rugged, he was trained, and in condition.

Mike picked up his history textbook, his favorite subject. He would work hard to catch up by concentrating during the holiday. He went into the bathroom and filled the tub with hot water.

He removed his clothing and eased into the bath.

Then he reached for his book. The water felt wonderful. Mike could soak out the pain and the fear.

Across the Santa Monica Mountains from the school Kathy Nelson emerged from her Junior League meeting in Westwood Village, searching for the family car. It was nowhere in sight. Instead, Jimmy Nye was grinning from behind the wheel of his Porsche. He reached over and opened the door.

"Your folks said you were here so I offered to pick you up," he said.

"Well, thanks." Kathy took a seat.

Nye drove slowly toward her home. "How's the little debutante?"

"I made my debut years ago and you know it."

"I was there," he said. "In fact, I was your escort."

"I know," she told him. "And where is Bobo today?"

"Never mind about Bobo. I'm interested in you."

"You can stop being interested in me."

He was silent, navigating traffic. Then he said bitterly, "I see your headline-hunting friend made it big in Kitzinger's story. He'll love that."

"The trouble with you, Jimmy, is that you can't stand seeing anyone else make good," Kathy said.

"I don't understand you, Kathy. How can you hang around with that character?"

The car stopped at a traffic light on Wilshire Boulevard. Kathy opened the door and slid out. Slamming it,

48

she said, "Thanks for the lift. I hope Ohio State beats you to pieces."

She walked briskly toward a taxi stand. There was never a cab waiting, but she could use the telephone to call one. She was seething with anger.

Yet she wondered, while waiting, why she did like Mike Caron. He certainly wasn't the kind of boy she had grown up with. Maybe that was the reason. She smiled to herself. Mike was different. He had drive and ambition, courage and fortitude.

Bob Westover was Mike's friend. That meant a lot. Everyone knew the kind of man Bob was . . . the best. If he thought enough of Mike to room with him, if they had been so close through the years, there could be nothing wrong with Mike. Kathy only wished he were less insecure, less worried about the future, less moody.

She didn't realize Bob, too, sometimes had his reservations about Mike.

5

THE WINTER MONTHS went by without snow,
without freeze, with the monotony of the school grind.
Bob Westover was a worried young man. Mike Caron
had not been himself since the day of the picnic and
the accident at cliffside. The injury affected Mike's
moods, driving him to abysmal depths.

Bob went to the first spring-practice football session
alone. As captain he had great responsibilities. Coach
Randolph was a stern taskmaster, a fretful soul.

The odor of the dressing room was, as always, pun-
gent with liniment and leather, exciting, stimulating.
Bob opened his locker, undressed slowly, donning running shorts, athletic socks, a sweat shirt and shoes with
cleats. Next to his locker was one marked, "Caron
#17." It stood closed, unlike the others that were being
used.

Again Bob thought of Mike's behavior during the
past weeks. Mike's sullen moodiness had been hard

enough to take. The cold shoulder extended to friend and roommate was worse. He hoped that by some miracle Mike would be able to pass the annual physical, but he doubted seriously whether this would occur. If Mike lost his athletic career he would be impossible to get along with.

Dan Kyle, the tall, studious quarterback, came in and said, "Well, captain, how does it look?"

"Haven't made up my mind," Bob answered. "Have you?"

"I've read and reread the schedule. We open against Michigan. We close against USC. What's in between can send us all to the funny factory."

"Stanford, Oregon State, Washington, U.C.L.A., California, Notre Dame, Texas, and Ohio State," Bob said, reeling them off like a television announcer. "We didn't only go big time. We went super time."

"If we win half of them we should get a special award," suggested Kyle. "Like, for showing up."

Seriously, Bob commented, "We've got the men. We've got the coaching. Can we stick in there week after week?"

"That's the question." Kyle shrugged. "How's Mike?"

"All right. He's due any minute."

"A lot depends on Mike. He's the break-away guy."

Behind them a cheerful voice asked, "What about me?"

Joe Danning stood there grinning at them.

"You, too," said Kyle without smiling. "McGill and

Bowers will do their part. You'll get blocking from them and from Morgan and Heiss. Make sure you follow them."

Danning said, "Gimme that key block and I'll get you six, every time." He looked at Bob. "Coach wants to see you."

"Okay. See you later," said Bob, going toward Randolph's office. He wondered what Danning had been doing, closeted with Randolph before the others arrived. Again he worried about Mike. It was no secret that the head coach had no great fondness for his star ground-gainer. Danning was a junior this season and entitled to a full trial. More problems for Mike Caron.

Coach Randolph was not alone in the big office adjoining the gymnasium. Mike Tilden, backfield coach, and Knox Dillon, who handled the line, plus several assistants, were in evidence. So were the student manager and Dean Madison, of the SFU Athletic Association. A meeting of the brass. The air was full of grim significance. For a fleeting moment Bob remembered his father sighing, "Football is no longer played for fun. You have to really love it to give it all that blood, sweat, and tears."

Randolph was asking, "Where is Caron?"

"He was to take his medical," answered Bob. "He should be here by now."

"Is there anything wrong with him?"

"Not that I know of," said Bob, poker faced. This was true enough; he wished he knew more.

"Then why is he late?"

"Why don't you ask him?" Bob was resentful.

Randolph cleared his throat. "Well, you are his roommate, you know. And you're team captain. Thought you might help us out. Caron will carry a big load next season."

"I imagine he'll be around in the fall," Bob told them.

"Sure, and still a problem. He'll always be a problem." Randolph scowled. "We want you to impress Caron with the seriousness of his position. We want you to work with him on formations, on following the plays. It's important, Westover."

"Whatever you say, coach."

Randolph peered suspiciously from beneath beetled brows. "I know you're good friends, went through high together, all that. Nevertheless, I expect results."

"Of course, coach. I understand," said Bob.

"You're one of our bulwarks. I appreciate your value and your influence. And so do the players."

"I don't quite understand what you mean."

"Well, Caron and others depend a lot upon you." The coach seemed a bit unsure of himself, as if he did not dare say precisely what he meant.

"I see," said Bob. He waited. Uncomfortable silence reigned.

Then Mike Caron walked into the room, an envelope in his hand. He quickly sensed the strained atmosphere, grinned. He winked at Bob, walked slowly past him, and laid the envelope before Randolph.

"Something up, gents?" he asked with affected innocence.

"You're late," growled the coach.

"Your doctor gave me a hard time," Mike told him.

"Did you pass the physical?" Randolph was sarcastic.

"Just barely." Mike held out his hand, palm down. "Hangnails, you know. And some dandruff, but they say there's a television ad about that, how you can cure it and be beautiful for the prom."

Randolph's dislike of Mike, thought Bob, was hard to conceal. There simply was no empathy between the two. A team captain had to worry about situations like that.

Randolph was snapping, "Dress and try some sprints. I'm going to drive you men as you've never been driven before. This is my year and we're going to take every advantage of it."

"Your year? Or the team's year?" asked Mike. Bob thought he heard the coach mutter an uncomplimentary reply. They went back to the locker room. The entire squad had arrived amid much noise and confusion. The roommates made their way to their adjoining cubicles.

"Coach was on my back, wasn't he?"

Bob answered, "In a way. On mine, also."

"With that schedule, he'll be foaming at the mouth from now until the twenty-seventh of November."

That was the date of the finale with USC. Bob grunted.

"We'll be bruised and battered before then. Well, we wanted to be football heroes."

"Didn't we, though? Remember in high school, how we used to dream about it?"

"And we made it."

Mike donned his shorts. "Yeah. We made it." He fell silent, his face clouded again.

Bob knew this mood. He said, "See you on the field of glory."

He went outdoors. The sun was shining hotly down on the practice field. Springtime in southern California was like summertime in other climes. A lot of lard would be sweated off football candidates this season.

They came straggling out, big ones, smaller ones—but no little ones. They were a husky lot. In the short period of its existence, San Fernando University had attracted an amazing number of top prospects from prep schools and junior colleges. Randolph had organized well and the jump into the big time was not as dangerous as might appear.

Bob joined the sprinters under an assistant with a starter's pistol. At the far end of the gridiron was another coach with a stop watch and a chart on which he would keep track of the speed of the aspirants. It was a matter of pride to Bob, the captain, that none of the linemen could make better time down the field than he. He stepped to the mark, took off, and fled over the turf.

It was odd, he thought, that he had suffered no ill

effects from the fall over the cliff. The pinched nerve had never given him another moment's trouble.

But Mike had had no such luck, he knew. Despite his denials, there was something wrong with Mike's right leg. Bob, forgetting about Mike, finished the run, heard the timer call out congratulations, turned and trotted back upfield.

Mike was getting set to run. Bob froze, watching. His concern returned. This was Mike's first test. So well had he concealed the injury that no one else was paying any attention to him when the gun went off.

Mike set sail. He seemed to move without effort, without pain. If he was a bit slower than last year it was not apparent.

Could he be mistaken, Bob wondered? If Mike weren't hurt, what about the times Bob had seen Mike wince when making certain moves in their room?

Bob went to the line, awaiting further instructions from the coaching staff. Time would tell. No use anticipating trouble. He could not believe, however, that Mike was fully hale and healthy.

Coach Randolph had work laid out on a minute-by-minute schedule. It was run and work and run and work, to prepare for as tough a season as any football team would face that year.

There were men for the job, though, Bob mused. His was a veteran team, with all the skills. The defensive front four of Tillou, Brown, Miller, and Ambrose, with Bob himself shuttling in and out as needed, averaged over two hundred and forty pounds. The linebackers and defensive wings and safeties were fleet and strong.

On offense there was Dan Kyle with the violinist's hands and the cool brain, a fine, inspiring quarterback. There was Con McGill, a flanker of note with Sam Ritz backing him, almost as skilful. Bill Bowers, a mammoth, bruising fullback and Tug Manning to spell him, were equally invaluable.

And there was Mike Caron.

And Joe Danning.

The offensive line was big and steady and knowledgeable, from Foran at center through the tackles. Morgan and Heiss were agile, powerful big ends. Their subs were more than adequate.

Coach Randolph had brought this squad up by hand. Many of them were scholarship boys, working their way through, though a surprising number were not. Almost all of them were California bred, a good many from the San Fernando Valley, where the university was located.

This was their year of trial. Mike Caron realized that. He ran with the others, then gathered for the lecture. He had found himself, luckily, able to move straight ahead as well as ever.

He had not attempted to change direction while at speed. He was well aware that his leg might buckle under such a move. He wondered why he bothered. Sooner or later it would prove out. They would be scrimmaging in another week or so. Why had he tried to make it?

For pride and fear, he ventured.

Bob Westover watched his roommate closely throughout the first afternoon. They had no chance to exchange words. Practice was too intense for chitchat. But Bob could see that Mike was preoccupied, worried. Several times Randolph asked questions that Mike was slow in answering.

Joe Danning had the answers. He was quick to give them. Quick afoot, too, sprinting nimbly up and down the field all afternoon. A very good halfback, was Joe Danning.

But, Bob thought, Joe's not a likeable character. He seems to have no close friends, indeed few acquaintances. He's a bit too pushy, too aggressive, too cocky.

Coach Randolph, of course, had no interest in Danning's personality. He could only see that the junior running back had talent and might back up Mike Caron well.

Spring-practice session promised to be exciting.

6

ON THE DAY OF scrimmage electric tension ran through the SFU locker room. The veterans laughed and indulged in horseplay among themselves, but they felt the tension as much as the greenest rookie. All else up to now had been preparation. Now was the time to butt heads. Today the sheep would be separated from the goats. Some players would be relegated to the White Shirts, or told that big-time football was not for them, not here, not against this array of talent.

Bob Westover felt oddly apart from what was going on. He watched Mike don the pads, bit his lip to refrain from saying what was uppermost in his mind. There had been little exchange between them, truthfully, in the past days, since he had hinted strongly that Mike should give up football for the year. Bob had been shut up with a sharp, crackling reminder to mind his own business.

Mike saw Coach Randolph approaching and sensed

trouble. He braced himself and pulled on his jersey, facing the coach.

Randolph said in low tones, "I wanted to take you two on together, since you're such friends."

"I stand on my own feet," snapped Mike.

Randolph stiffened. "You do, at that. You stand on them. But you're not moving very well on them."

"I move well enough."

"You've been loafing and you know it. You haven't been listening to half of what the coaching staff has been saying. Your attitude has been, in plain words, lousy."

Mike said, "You shouldn't judge my attitude. Just let action on the field talk for itself, why don't you?"

Bob shook his head sadly. "Mike, I'm afraid I know what the coach means."

"You, too!" Mike's face was flushed. "Why don't you all mind your own business?"

"Because we're worried," Randolph confessed. "You were to be the star this year. You were to be All America. The team, the school, the coaches all depended upon that."

"That's right, Mike. Everyone's on your side." Bob was pleading.

"I don't need anyone on my side. Just let the line open a few holes, give me a key block, and I'll do the rest."

"If they're not on your side, why should they block for you?" demanded Randolph. "You seldom have a civil word for anyone. You never consult with me. What's got into you, anyway?"

"I'm here on a scholarship to play football," Mike told him. "I know the signals. Let's get out there and see whether I can do the job, shall we?"

He stomped out, cleats scratching on the cork floor. Randolph stared after him, then turned to Bob.

"Well?"

"I don't know what's with him," Bob confessed. "I just don't know."

"He doesn't confide in you?"

"No, he doesn't."

"Something's eating him. He's acting very strangely. If he doesn't improve . . . I don't know what I'll do. There's Danning, but he's also flakey. I'm beginning to think this is the year for temperamental running backs."

"I wish I had the answer, coach."

"Otherwise, the team is solid," mused Randolph. "It could be a great season. But if our break-away back fails us, they'll blitz on every play. They'll break up Kyle's pass patterns, upset our rhythm. Caron always was a wild man but I thought as a senior he'd come into his own."

"He was the best we ever had," Bob said.

"He was." Randolph started. "That's it . . . he was."

Bob sat for a moment, worrying, wondering. He had told Randolph everything he knew, up to a point. He dared not mention something was wrong with Mike's right leg. That was, as Mike had pointed out, Mike's own business.

Bob got up after a while and went out into the hot sun. California football players are accustomed to hot weather but this day promised to be a scorcher. The coaches were giving out instructions and final line-ups.

Randolph said, "I want Tillou, Brown, Miller and . . ." he hesitated, then added, "Westover up front on defense. Gould will be middlebacker. The corners, Killeen and Osmanski . . . no, check that . . . Danning, I want you to try defense for awhile in place of Osmanski."

Danning flashed Randolph a startled look. His green eyes narrowed. Then he grinned, spat on his hands.

"Offense will be last year's starters. You all know your positions," Randolph continued, finishing the selections for the afternoon. "The ball will be taken on the twenty-yard line. You all attempt to move it. I want all tackles sharp and clean but no pile-ups. And I want the offense to go all out. Who begins next fall will be decided on your work today and the rest of this week, remember that."

Coach tossed the ball to an assistant and went to the specially constructed tower from which he watched with the aid of field glasses, noting every player in turn, missing nothing.

Bob bumped shoulder pads with Asher Brown, a Negro two hundred and forty-five pounder. "Well, here we go again."

"It should be good, it should be very good."

62

"It's nice to work together again," Bob said.

"It's always nice to work," repeated Brown. "I love this game, Bob."

"I know you do."

They lined up. The front four spaced themselves, behemoths all. Linebackers poised, awaiting the offensive players' choice of spots into which, before the snap back, linemen would leap, according to which side Dan Kyle posted his flanker back and tight end. Bob Westover stood tall, watching, ready.

Kyle knew better than to begin with tricky play. He counted off, then handed the ball to big, tough Bill Bowers. Bob fought his way to the blocker, who happened to be Mike Caron. Asher Brown stopped the play inside for a two-yard gain. Mike got up without a word or a look and ran back to the huddle. The defense men gathered around Bob, but it was Asher Brown who gave the signals to them. They nodded and took their places.

Kyle looked them over, calmly called. Bob knew a change of signals was taking place but had to guess in which direction. He got a pretty good jump on Foran's snap back to Kyle and began working his way in.

When Mike faced him, blocking, Bob yelled, "Pass! Pass!"

He brushed Mike aside and went for Kyle, who had gone straight back into the pocket. In that instant Bob knew he should have paid more heed to his roomie. He ran into Bowers, and before he could untangle himself

Kyle cocked his arm, faked, spun, and threw softly over the line into the flat.

Mike took the ball over his shoulder and kept right on running, never pausing or looking back. No one was fleet enough to give him a start on an angle. He completed a touchdown play and Randolph whistled them off the chase.

"All right," said the coach. "That was just the way it should be done. Perfect. Can't blame the defense. Let's try it again, Kyle."

The players went back to the twenty-yard line to begin again. The defense, despite absolution by the boss, was smarting. Bob scowled, scanning the line-up as Kyle brought the offense unit into formation. It should be another slant, he thought, with Mike carrying. Brown thought so, too, and gave a little toward the middle of the line.

Bowers rushed. Kyle had an annoying habit of repeating a pattern and fooling the opposition. There were no grooves in the quarterback's organized mind. Bowers got four yards.

In the huddle, Asher said earnestly, "That man upsets me. You think he'll pass again?"

"I think he'll run," Bob offered.

"He won't pass in my zone," Danning bragged. "I'd have had Caron if he'd been in my zone."

No one replied. Brown signaled.

Again Kyle stepped back. This time he dealt a quick look-in to his flanker, Con McGill. The ball nestled in the veteran's arms. He spun. Danning, coming viciously and low, was eager to be noticed. McGill crossed over and walked out of the embrace, going for the side lines and the blockers.

Bob Westover shoved Mike Caron out of his way, took off flying. He got one hand on McGill. One hand was enough as Asher Brown crashed.

But the gain was eight yards and the defense backed up to the thirty-two. Danning was mumbling, "I slowed him down, didn't I? Couldn't get a clean shot. . . ."

Brown gently interrupted, "I think fifty-two this time."

This was the defense against the tackle slant. Kyle had gone straight ahead twice. Now the linebackers pretended to set against this maneuver. At the last moment, however, they shifted outside, left and against the strong alignment.

Kyle faked to Bowers. Then he handed off to Mike Caron. Bob lunged in, his assignment to keep the play confined within the ends. The tough Sandy Gould plugged the hole made by Foran and Pascal on their charge. Brown and Bob pinched in as Mike took the ball and whizzed for the hole that was not there.

They went down in a heap, Mike underneath the pile. No gain. They quickly peeled off and Mike, hesitating slightly, got to his feet.

Asher said, "That got 'em. Now look out for the pass."

Bob was more wary. He lined up with his eyes on Kyle, then on Mike. Kyle sometimes used a counter play. This was almost the same as the previous one, but an entrapment and a slight delay were involved, which let Kyle pitch out to Mike. That would allow him running room to make his sparkling cut wherever he saw daylight in the defense.

At the last moment Bob wheeled off, looking for this play. He saw Danning come up from the defensive wing to protect the inside. He saw Kyle make his first fake, then another. Mike was coming fast, taking the underhand toss from Kyle.

Danning tried to get into position, but Bowers slammed him aside. At the same moment Pascal, the running guard, lowered his round head and hammered at Bob.

For a split instant the hole was wide. All Mike had to do was make his cut to get into it. No one could have prevented him from making another first down. Bob fought Pascal, intending to follow the play, in case anyone slowed down Mike.

Then Mike was on the ground. Bob saw it all. As his roommate tried to cross over, his right leg buckled. As if shot he went down. Danning pounced on him.

Randolph came over, blowing the whistle, descending from the tower, stalking. "There was a hole big enough to accommodate the whole backfield. Where were you, Caron?"

Mike got up slowly. "Couldn't get into it."

Randolph said crisply, "I want to see that play again. At full speed."

Bob took a good look at Mike's expression. His

face was set in hard lines, seemed a dozen years older. The teams resumed their formations.

To run a play against a defense that's aware it is coming is a coach's dangerous gambit. It could teach a lesson or it could result in harm to a player's ego, or to his body.

Kyle began again. Bowers hit Danning, who came flying in. Bob was checked momentarily. Mike set his jaw and tried once more to make his cut. With super-human effort, Bob threw Pascal away from him and drove into Mike's path, trying to reach him before the leg gave out.

He failed. His fingers brushed Mike's pants. Mike sat down, clutching at his right thigh, letting the football bound away into Danning's eager arms.

Now Randolph was frightened. The trainer came running. A call was made to Doctor Raymond. Mike was helped off the field. Bob, heart heavy, went with him.

Mike's career is over, he kept thinking. The injury was bad. Mike had thought he could overcome it, but had found he could not make his cuts. As long as he ran straight ahead, witness the touchdown run, Mike seemed to be all right. But he could not change direction. A halfback who can't change direction is no halfback at all.

Joe Danning ran into the backfield, replacing Mike. The squad returned to work.

On the first play Danning tried to get fancy, lost his blockers. Bob took satisfaction in slamming him to the ground for a loss. Then he grew angry at himself. Being mean to Joe wouldn't bring Mike back.

Bob sweated out the remainder of the scrimmage, switching to offense for awhile to check his timing. He kept an eye on Danning, hoping against hope that Joe would settle down, learn what he had to before the USC game. When the whistle blew to announce the end of the session Bob headed straight for the locker room and began to dress. He wanted to get to Mike as soon as possible.

Before he had finished, Mike appeared, head too high, neck too rigid, eyes too bright. Bob's heart sank. "What is it?"

"They say I'll need surgery."

"We'll talk to my father about that."

"An operation could lame me."

"Dad will know. . . ."

"I've been keeping this from you, Bob. I've seen other doctors during the winter."

"Were they specialists?"

"I can't afford specialists. One suggested therapy. I think I'll take him up on it. I'm afraid to go on the table. I've got from now through summer to work out."

"Without consulting a surgeon?"

"Look, pal, I told you I can't afford a specialist."

"Dad will do it for you."

"Nothing doing."

"You've got to let us help."

"I've taken enough help from you, from everybody."

"That's crazy."

"Maybe. But that's how it goes, amigo."

"Mike, you're not being fair to yourself or any of us."

Caron was stiff and pale, his voice low and firm. "All right, I'm wrong. But I've thought it out and decided I just can't accept more charity from you. I can't do it. I'll work out of this my own way."

Bob glanced around. Other players were listening. Mike's voice had carrying power. "I'll talk to you in our room, amigo. You've got to listen to reason."

"I told you how I feel."

"We're discussing your whole future. Your life."

"Yeah, you said it. My life." Mike grinned, turned and walked out. Everybody noticed the limp.

"Why, Mike's hurt bad," Joe Danning said.

Bob laced his shoes and hurried to the dormitory. He stared at the note taped to their door.

Sorry, my friend. I have to work this out for myself. No charity, no loans. That's my religion. Thank you for everything. . . . Mike.

Clothing, books, were gone. Mike Caron had removed himself from the collegiate scene.

7

MIKE CARON PAUSED in front of 1112 Duveen
Street. His leg ached. He stared at the paper's clas-
sified section, then at the house number, then reread
the ad. *Room in house with Italian lady, enquire Mrs.
Pia Caruso.* He limped up the flower-bordered walk
and rang a push-button bell.

After a moment the door opened. A round-faced,
round-bodied woman wearing a clean, fitted housedress
surveyed him, smiling tentatively. She had white hair
pulled back tight. Her eyes were brown and wide and
amazingly youthful.

"I read your ad in the paper," said Mike. "You're
Mrs. Caruso?"

"Mama Pia," she said, her smile widening, warming. "You are Italiano, no?"

"I am Italiano, yes," Mike said. "Mike Caron."

"Come in, come in!" She stepped back. There was
no hallway. They entered directly into a sitting room

full of comfortable chairs. Though the carpet showed signs of wear, there was a television set in a corner, and small tables scattered for convenience. Everything was clean. A dining room could be seen beyond and past that a hallway leading to the rooms in the rear. Mike glanced into the white-tiled kitchen to the right. It was full of brass-bottomed pots and pans. A big electric refrigerator and a gas stove filled an entire corner.

"I need to rent a room," Mike said.

"What else?" She beamed. "Mike Caron. A good name. You know, you are the first to answer? That is luck. The very first, an Italiano boy."

"I have no idea what the price should be. I don't have a job and I don't know what I can pay."

"Pay? Ha!" she said. The smile seemed a part of her. "You like the pasta, eh?"

"I wasn't figuring on eating in. You see, I have to study a lot, keep up my studies for school in the fall. I don't know what my hours will be."

She said, "I only ask, you like the pasta?"

Now he found himself grinning back at her. "I'm an Italiano. I love the pasta."

She said, "Ten dollars a week? I keep the room and do your linens. When you want the pasta, I cook."

"That's a real bargain."

Mama Pia said, "Look, Italiano boy, I am widow. My son, Mario, he is in Viet Nam. My daughter, Maria, she is in New Jersey with four bambinos. It is lonely here. Why do they call me Mama Pia? Because I need young people, without young people the world is gray. So I put the ad in the paper and I pray for a young one, girl or boy. Just send me a young one. You come, I am happy. I am repaid."

"I'm not a very happy young one, Mrs. Caruso."

"Ah, so much the better! And it is 'Mama Pia,' not Mrs. Caruso. And when do you move in, Michael?"

"Any time. Now, today. I have only clothing and books."

She said, "Today! That is good! But you have not even seen your room! What a circumstance, we talk, we jabber, we do not look at the room. It was Mario's room, you understand. Come!"

He followed her down the hall, past the kitchen. In the rear she opened a door. The bathroom was conveniently opposite, he noted. He stepped into the medium-sized room behind Mama Pia. It was outfitted with a double bed and a side table with a reading lamp and bookshelves. There was a well-worn easy chair and a straight chair. The closet was a walk-in. A portable television set and a small radio occupied the bureau top. The single window was a wide one, overlooking a back yard garnished with dichondra grass and blossoms of pink and yellow and red and blue. Mike sank into the chair, stretching his aching leg in front of him at full length. "Ten dollars is not enough."

"You got so much money, then?"

"I have very little. And no job. You could easily get a better tenant."

"Pooh!" The warm smile widened. "You are the first,

72

you are Italiano. Ten dollars is what I want, no more. It is all decided. You want to bring in pasta, meatballs, you have enough, I cook. You no got, I feed. You go now and get your things, you stay with Mama Pia."

There was no resisting her. In a cold world, a new and strange world, she offered kindness. Mike arose and said, "Here's the ten for the first week. And I thank you."

"Pooh, thank me! Do not be too hasty. I am a nosey old woman. Maybe you get sick and tired of me some day. Go, now, and hurry back."

He went out into the hot sunshine. He was staggered by his luck in finding this remarkable woman and her comfortable haven. This was the first thing that had worked out for him since the disastrous picnic in the hills. Mike fingered the few bills left in his money clip. He limped to La Brea Avenue and waited for a bus, leaning against a post, studying the want ads. The first thing to do was find himself a job.

There seemed to be absolutely nothing for which he was qualified. Computer operators, technicians, college graduates, always college graduates were in demand. Salesmen on commission—he knew enough about himself to realize he would never make a good salesman. He could not even work in a shoe shop, because his leg would not permit getting up and down all day. He picked out an ad run by an employment agency. When the bus came along he rode it to Hollywood Boulevard and found the proper building and presented himself to a blonde, impersonal young woman.

73

He did not qualify for any of the jobs listed with the agency. The young woman frowned, said, "Try the State Employment Bureau."

Mike returned to the cheap hotel, checked out. He would try the state later. Panic was again eating him. He hauled his textbooks and clothing down to the cab stand and directed the driver to 1112 Duveen Street.

Mama Pia was waiting. She seized his clothing and made off with it while he was paying the driver. He carried books and suitcases to the rear room, where both busied themselves arranging his possessions. Mama Pia chattered all the while. Mike kept silent, fighting his fear, polishing his stubbornness.

He would not give in. He had renounced SFU, at least temporarily, his friends there. Memory of his grandfather's lifelong indebtedness rode him like a cement collar. He had to make it on his own, earn the money to get well first, then back into school, any school, anywhere, if SFU wouldn't have him, so that he could get a degree and better himself in the world without football.

He knew, now, that he would never play professional football, any football. SFU had given him the football scholarship. If he couldn't play why would they want him? This he had accepted. His only hope lay in surgery. But he would not submit to surgery without a guarantee that he would be able to walk with full freedom. And he would pay in full for that guarantee. Otherwise he would try to get well through exercise. He would do for himself, without charity from others. There was no other course.

He had pain but he would ignore the pain. He limped, but he was stronger than most men. His arms and shoulders were powerful. He would find work and he would prevail.

Mama Pia sensed Mike's preoccupation. She left him alone. He sat in the chair, thinking, somber.

He had sent Kathy a note. He had told her he wouldn't see her this summer, that his course of action would not allow him spare time.

What he really meant was that he would not permit Kathy or Bob Westover or any of his former friends to help with his problem. This was something he had to do by himself, without their knowledge or consent.

Mike's leg hurt. It was afternoon, too late to begin the search for employment. He picked up a book. He had laid out a course of study with the aid of university program notes. He would not fall behind, he told himself. If he couldn't go back to SFU he'd try for another college, a less expensive one. He would not accept aid, nor would he borrow.

The college, the other world of which he had been a part, seemed a thousand miles away.

Alongside the family swimming pool, Kathy Nelson lay in the sun with Nancy Waite, not hearing the transistorized music that filled the air, scarcely hearing what Nancy was telling her.

"Bob hasn't heard a word from Mike. No one has. I declare, I can't imagine what got into him. He just dropped out of everything."

"Not out of the world," Kathy answered. "He's somewhere, trying to do something. Whether he's right or wrong, he's working out something."

"You weren't so sure a few weeks ago."

"I'm not sure of anything."

"You're sure you're having a lousy summer. You mope. You talk to yourself. You ignore Jimmy. By the way, he broke off with Bobo."

"I heard," Kathy said. "He's coming for dinner with Bob tonight. My folks invited him."

"He is?" Nancy perked up. "Say, fun for a change. Jimmy's good for you. He can make you laugh."

"Big deal," murmured Kathy. Her yellow hair was white in the sun.

"You can't mourn all summer for Mike. Life's too short," Nancy told her. "If he turns up again, that's another matter. Meantime, this is our last vacation as schoolgirls. You know that. We'll be out in the world next year."

"You'll be married to Bob," Kathy predicted. "Medical school won't stop him from asking you."

"Maybe I will. Maybe not," said Nancy. "I can't decide. Maybe he'd be better off waiting until he's through with school."

"Then he'll be an intern. Why wait?"

"Want to do the right thing. Meantime, we have this wonderful summertime to enjoy."

"Yes," said Kathy without enthusiasm. "Don't we, though?"

Mike's last note had been so cold, so strange. She could feel him removing himself from her life. She had tried hard to convince herself that perhaps this was all for the best. Her heart would not accept her argument. Her heart, in fact, had objected violently. Undying love was corny, old-fashioned, she'd reasoned. Today's women were practical, down to earth, realistic. If modern, why did she wake up at night worrying about a beetle-browed, black-haired roughneck named Mike Caron?

Why did she, indeed? She'd have a lot of good times with Jimmy Nye and Bob and Nancy if she'd forget Mike. Why must she think about a boy who had left her with a curt note, not even a good-bye meeting?

Was it because she knew, or at least suspected that Mike could not face her without cracking? Was it because despite the fact she thought he was wrong, she respected him for trying to make it entirely on his own?

She had no ready answers. She only knew that when trunk-clad Jimmy strutted into the pool area, with a flip word and a graceful dive into the water, she felt nothing, absolutely nothing. She looked up at Bob Westover with a question in her eyes.

He shook his head. "Not a word from him."

"Can't we hire a detective or something?" She spoke without thinking, out of frustration.

"Can you imagine what would happen?"

She smiled without mirth. "He'd kill us."

77

"He sure wouldn't like it," Bob said. "He has to do it his way . . . everything."

"You're angry with him, aren't you?"

"No, not angry."

"Just hurt?"

"Not hurt. Annoyed, I guess," Bob said. "I think he's acting like a fool. A chump. A stubborn idiot."

"But it's his decision," she pointed out. "He has a right."

"Yes," said Bob reluctantly, "he has a right to live his life . . . the wrong way."

The extension phone tinkled and Kathy went to it. A voice said, "Kathy?"

"Mike!"

"Are you alone?"

Jimmy had emerged from the pool and was looking for her. She answered, "No, I'm not. Where are you?"

"Don't mention my name again. Just meet me. At Hollywood and Vine. Can you?"

"When?" Her pulse was rapid, her face flushed.

"When can you make it? Now?"

"It'll take at least an hour."

"All right. An hour. In front of the Broadway."

"But . . ." He had hung up. He must be in trouble, she thought. She left the phone, collecting her wits. She said to the others, "That was my cousin, Marge. Something's come up. I have to leave."

"But what about dinner?" Nancy demanded.

"You take care of everything. There are steaks for

78

the barbecue. I'll try and be back." She was already moving toward the house. She would have to shower and put on her new summer dress and. . . .

Jimmy called, "Some date, you are! Crazy!"

"I'm sorry. Youall have fun." She was running for the house, her mind full of many things.

Mike Caron walked slowly up and down in front of the department store at the famed intersection of Hollywood Boulevard and Vine Street. This meeting ground was far enough from his new home yet not too far to reach without much cost. He had called Kathy on impulse, because he felt guilty, and because he thought he might explain himself to her. Now he was not sure that he had acted correctly, that it would work out for him or for her.

The little car arrived. He got into it, with some difficulty. Kathy drove expertly toward Sunset Boulevard.

He said, "You look great."

"Thanks. You look pretty bad."

"I know."

She pulled up at a red light. "Where do we go?"

"Just drive around," he told her. "I haven't any money. I'm working but they haven't paid me as yet."

"Where are you working?"

"Oh . . . on a job."

"You won't talk, eh?" She tried to make a joke of it.

"Talk won't help."

"Then why did you call me?"

"Just to . . . I wanted to see you."

She drove up a side street and parked, then turned and looked at him. "Driving around is no good. What is it, Mike? What's wrong?"

"Nothing," he insisted. He could not, after all, explain. It would sound like excuses, apologies.

She got out of the car and said, "Let's walk a bit. We used to talk things out, walking."

He swung out, hampered by his bad leg. He realized she was watching as he rounded her side of the car. He failed to notice an upended spot in the walk. He tripped, tried to catch himself, swung around as his leg gave way.

He sat down hard on the walk, hurt. He stared up at her. She bent to him, reaching. "Mike! Oh, Mike!"

"Get away from me. Don't touch me." He was deep in anguish, distress, shame. "Just go away. Get in your car and beat it."

"No. Let me help you." She reached urgently for him.

He thrust his hands savagely at her. "I said go away. Leave me alone. Get away from here!"

Her panic faded, her own anger rose. "Mike, one more time. Let me help you."

"I don't want your help."

"All right. I'll go. Stay there and feel sorry for yourself. Stay there and rot in your stupid stubborn way!"

She turned and ran for the car.

He pushed himself to his feet. He heard the car start but did not look at Kathy. He waited until she had engaged the gears and departed. He made three steps to a tree and leaned hard against it. He had tried and he had failed. Now he was really alone.

8

THE JOB WAS one that no one else had wanted that day at the State Employment Office. Mike soon found out why. He would be a helper on an independently owned trash-collecting truck for fifty dollars per week.

The driver was a huge Negro named Charlie Boone. The other man on the back of the truck was José Garcia, who was small and light but very quick. Mike liked his new companions. The work, however, was hard and dirty.

They started early in the morning and if there were calls after the regular route they worked late, for which they received no overtime. PICK-UPCO was nonunion. If the help didn't like the pay, they could quit, the owner said. Martin Granger, a husky blond man with a mustache, had one walleye, which made him look ferocious.

The city collected garbage, but not trash. People paid for this service, especially in the Wilshire district where the big truck went up and down the streets day after day, week after week.

He was not in danger of being recognized, Mike realized at once. Even if anyone he knew lived in this area, no one ever really looked at the trash collectors, really looked at him. He was as anonymous as an unsigned letter.

Mike believed lugging the trash, emptying it, hopping on and off the back of the truck would be good for his leg. At least, he'd be exercising. On his first Saturday off, he was dragging out of his room and into the kitchen when Mama Pia finally spoke.

"You don't want to talk about the leg, eh?"

For a moment he was angry. Then he swallowed coffee, coughed, said mildly, "I don't like to talk about it, no."

"You got the bad leg, you don't want to mention it."

"That's right."

"But Mama Pia wants to mention it."

"All right. You mention it."

"Why you no go to the doctor?"

"I no got the money," he said, grinning.

"You go to the clinic, then. What's the matter you?"

"I've been to a doctor. He wanted to operate. He said I may not walk again if it didn't work."

She said, "You go to Doctor Smith." It was a pronouncement, as though everything had been decided.

"Doctor who?"

"Doctor Smith. He is best in the world. My son, Mario, he had fractured leg. Bad nerves, all messed up.

Doctor Smith," she repeated firmly. "He give us much time to pay."

A bell rang in Mike's memory. "Would that be Ransom Smith?"

"Yes. Doctor Ransom Smith."

"He's the most expensive in the state."

Mama Pia said, "Not for poor folks, he ain't."

"I'm not taking charity," Mike told her flatly. "I am not going into debt. If I can save enough, I'll try your Doctor Smith. Okay?"

Mama Pia started to protest, stopped. She looked hard and long at Mike. Then she lifted one expressive shoulder. "You be sorry, one day."

Nothing more was said that day. Mike spent the week end in his room reading, studying. He had no money to spend—and his leg hurt worse than ever.

Nothing was said about his limp on the job, either. Helpers at low pay were hard to find. Charlie Boone looked at him worriedly sometimes, but kept his mouth shut. Mike went about his tasks doggedly, enduring the pain.

It took Mike three weeks to accustom himself to the labor. He had saved a few dollars but his leg was no better. At about this time Charlie Boone became ill. Martin Granger was forced to take over the truck, a job he detested.

In the first place, Granger was a poor driver and didn't enjoy driving. He jerked the gear-shift and let the clutch out too quickly. Both the helpers were reeling on the back step. In the second place, Granger used his loud voice to let anyone within hearing know that he was the boss and the two helpers were dirt under his feet. Mike and José were hauling out a big batch of rubbish from a stately home on Arden Street near Wilshire when Granger became angrily impatient with the size of the job.

"All right, get the lead out. Jump!"

José staggered under a large unwieldy carton. Mike extended a hand to steady the load.

"All right, Caron, attend to your own job, you and that gimpy leg of yours," barked Granger. He came down off the truck and swaggered toward them. "Move!"

"Why don't you take a hand yourself if you're in such a rush?" Mike asked.

The boss howled, "Don't talk back to me, you crummy ginney."

The lady of the house, dressed for town, was going toward the Cadillac in the garage at the rear. She paused, smiling at the scene. Her smile faded.

Mike took two steps toward Granger, his leg buckling a little. Granger swung a wild punch at him, yelling, "You're fired."

Mike feinted with his left and dropped a right to Granger's nose. Blood spurted. The lady uttered a small cry. Mike hit the big man with a left and Granger went down and rolled on the lawn.

"I'm sorry to litter your grass like this," Mike told her. "Good-bye, now."

The lady came toward him, saying, "He shouldn't have done that."

"I know." Mike stared at Granger, who was scrabbling about but making no real effort to rise while Mike was still in the neighborhood. "I shouldn't be working for a man like that. Nobody should."

The lady said, "You'd better come with me. He'll probably want to call the police."

For once Mike did not hesitate. He accepted the offer, got into the Cadillac, and allowed the lady to drive him to the nearest bus stop. She said in parting, "If you have any trouble with him, let me know. My husband is a lawyer."

She gave him a card. The name was Harvey Desmond. He tucked the pasteboard away and went home. He dragged himself into Mama Pia's kitchen and told her what had happened.

"You can't be trash collector," she said. "Now you go to Doctor Smith."

"I haven't enough money."

"You go. I call him, you go and get fixed."

"No," said Mike. "I'll look for another job."

"When Granger, he gets through, the State Employment will think you are criminal," Mama Pia told him. "What kind of job can you do? Labor. Hard labor. What kind of job should you not do? Labor. Hard work. No, you go to Doctor Smith."

He shrugged. He needed a couple of hundred dollars before even thinking about going to Doctor Smith. Time was marching by, the summer would be running out. He didn't see now how he'd get back to school by fall. He said, "I need time, Mama Pia. I need more time."

At the corner lunchroom where he sometimes ate tasteless meals to avoid sponging off Mama Pia he was offered employment as a dish washer. He had to accept. He received free dinners and five dollars per week.

He began to panic, deep inside. There seemed no end to this vicious circle, no way to go, no sunshine ahead. He spent more and more time in his room, brooding. Mama Pia's pleasant face began to sadden.

Kathy was dancing with Jimmy Nye. Nancy and Bob were at the table in The Grove when a lady came to them and said, "Bob, how are you?"

He stood up. "Good evening, Mrs. Desmond. How are you?"

"I had a strange experience last week," she said. "I thought I recognized a young man, then imagined I was seeing things. Now I know I was right. Last time I saw him, he was with you. An Italian fellow."

"Mike!" said Bob. "It was Mike Caron."

"Dark, good looking. But this boy was working on a trash truck," she said, puzzled. "Is that a new way of keeping in shape for football?"

"Well. . . ."

"I saw him get fired," she said. "He punched his boss, a bully."

Bob asked, "What was the name of the company?"

She told him. "We got rid of the company after the incident. It seemed fair. They fired the young man. We fired them."

She smiled and left. Bob sat down and stared at Nancy. He said, "My father's lawyer is her husband."

"I wonder where Mike went when he left?"

"To a new job," Bob said. "Look, don't say anything in front of Jimmy, huh?"

She sighed. "I don't know why we stick by Mike, but we do. All of us."

"Especially Kathy."

They looked at her. Jimmy Nye was chattering like a magpie, trying to capture her attention. Kathy, a fixed smile on her face, was gazing over the crowd, at nothing.

"Especially Kathy," echoed Nancy.

By Monday they had checked out Mike's address through Martin Granger and were parked in the neighborhood, all three of them, watching. They saw Mike come out, limp down the street toward the bus stop on his way to look for work. They waited until the bus picked him up, then Bob approached Mama Pia's house and rang the bell.

Mama Pia asked, "Yes, who is it?"

"Friends of Mike."

She opened the door and some of the worry creases fled. "Friends? Ah, how he needs friends, my Michael."

Bob beckoned and the girls, scrutinized by Mama Pia, walked across the street. They sat down on porch chairs and examined one another.

Bob said, "He's limping worse than usual."

"And he has less money."

"We heard he lost his job."

"Such a job he had, for a lame boy!"

"We can't give him money," Bob said. "He's too stubborn."

"This is his name. Mister Stubborn," she agreed. "Doctor Smith, he is my friend, Michael will not go and see him."

They listened to her as she told them about Ransom Smith and the wonders he had worked. Bob pondered for a moment.

"You can trust this friend, Doctor Smith?"

"With my life," she exclaimed fervently.

"I'm sure my father knows him. Maybe we can work something out." Bob spoke slowly, trying to think. "Mike will accept anything he thinks he earns."

"That's right," said Kathy. "He's been trying to save to go to a doctor."

"Doctor Smith," nodded Mama Pia.

"Supposing Doctor Smith came to him?"

"But how?" they demanded in chorus.

"Well . . . supposing Doctor Smith had work that Mike could do. Something like that."

Saucer-eyed, Mama Pia stammered, "But he does . . . how did you know? He has the houses, the apartment house, the rental houses. He is buyer of land, houses. He believes in it. It is he who made us buy thisa house!"

Bob muttered, "This may be pointing to a change in luck for our boy, Mike."

"But how we do it?" demanded Mama Pia, all excited.

"I'll talk to my father," said Bob. He looked at the Italian lady. "I think Mike's luck changed when he found you."

"Luck? I do not know luck," she said. "I pray. I light the candle, as I do for my Mario in Viet Nam."

Kathy said, "Whatever did it, he came to the right place." She wiped away a tear. "Such a good place. You're a wonderful lady, Mama Pia."

"It is only that everyone should have a home," said Mama Pia gently. "Michael, he had no home."

"Only the school," Kathy said. "But he wouldn't stay. What was there left for him?"

The older woman shook her head, saying, "Our Michael, he is far from perfecto, sí? He had you. He knew not how to do with you. He is not good with people. He has a bad thing, a fear of taking help."

"He's afraid of owing anyone," Bob confirmed.

"Yes, that's Mike," Kathy agreed. "We'd better get out of here before he comes home."

"You'll hear from Doctor Smith," Bob promised as they arose. "My father will see to it."

"But Mike must never know," Kathy admonished.

"Just that he should have his poor leg fixed," Mama Pia said. "Just so he should have peace. In his soul."

90

They departed. They drove out to Westwood in the Mustang, not saying much, thinking a lot. Each felt hope, but also gnawing doubt. They knew Mike Caron and his ways.

A day later Mike Caron was sitting across the desk from Doctor Smith, answering questions. He was desperate, his money gone. He owed rent to Mama Pia. He needed work, he had to have work. The doctor's call had saved him.

"Yes," he was saying, "I went to college for three years."

"It shows." Doctor Ransom Smith was tall and thin, with long, tapering fingers that moved like snakes atop the desk. He seemed to want to use those fingers. He picked up a pencil. "Michael Caron. What college?"

"San Fernando U," said Mike reluctantly.

"Ah. I see. And when did you injure yourself?"

Mike said, "That's not the point, doctor. You want a handy man. I can do the job."

"Possibly. But workers must be insured," said the doctor. "Must have protection, you know."

"Well . . . I hadn't thought of that." Mike rose, with difficulty. The leg was getting worse every day. "I guess I won't do then?"

"Sit down, Caron." Doctor Smith had an open, surprisingly youthful face. He grinned, showing fine, white teeth. "You'll do."

Mike sat down. "I need the work, sir."

"I'm looking for an intelligent man to look after the properties, a reliable man to collect rents. There'll be some physical work, you understand, fixing faucets, minor plumbing, even some painting. And some book work. It would be worth a lot to get a college man. But on the insurance, we have to be in the clear. May I look at that leg?"

"No use, sir. They say I need surgery."

"I'm a surgeon."

Mike shook his head. "I have no money. And I will not accept charity. Never!"

"Who said anything about charity? I need a man, a whole man, a healthy man. All my funds are invested in real estate. Let me try and make a deal with you."

"No deals," Mike said. "I'll get along." He arose once more, turned too quickly. The leg buckled. He clutched the desk top with both hands, found himself looking into the doctor's compassionate eyes.

They stared at one another. Between them there passed a spark. Mike felt something tangible, as though he had touched a live wire.

Doctor Smith spoke quietly, "I said I needed a man. Are you man enough, Caron?"

"I've been wondering about that. They say surgery could leave me a cripple if it failed."

"I don't fail," said the doctor. "I accept only those cases I can guarantee. But I do require a thorough examination."

"You'll make a deal so that I can pay you?"

92

"Better trust me, hadn't you?"

Mike sighed. His heart lifted. "I'll try it. I'll try it. I think I can trust you, doc."

"Let's get on with it, then."

Mike went into the examining room and was tapped and prodded and X-rayed. A starched, middle-aged nurse impassively ordered him about to the doctor's satisfaction. When it was over Mike waited in the office for the report.

Doctor Smith was not long in joining him. His smile was wide. "You've really had a time, haven't you?"

"It's not been good."

"You have an injury that would fool a lot of doctors," said Smith. "Happens to be a specialty of mine. It's in the joint."

"They all said that. Said it was a dangerous operation."

"Not in my young life. Tricky but, would you believe it, a minor piece of work?"

"Minor?" Mike couldn't believe his ears.

"Tricky but minor. I won't bore you with long medical terms. A nerve and a muscle close to the hip joint are involved. That make sense?"

"It's too simple." Mike held his breath.

"You let me operate and you'll be as good as new in a week or so. You won't be able to make those quick stops and spins on a dance floor. But you'll be good enough to work for me."

"About the payment?" Mike's voice was strained.

"A promissory note," said Doctor Smith briskly. "You pay me, pay the hospital, everything, out of your salary."

"But that's . . . that's too generous."

"It's what I want," the doctor said gently. "Don't be foolish, this is a two-way deal. I'm not giving you anything. Your pay will be—oh, let's say eighty per week. I'll take thirty. Can you live on fifty?"

"I can and I will," said Mike. "I've been existing on less. When do we start?"

Doctor Smith scribbled on his pad. "You go to my private hospital this afternoon. The promissory note will be brought to you there. We will operate tomorrow."

Mike took the note, looked at it, rubbed his eyes, stared at Doctor Smith. "I can't believe this, sir. It's like . . . like God interfered. I don't deserve this."

"Forget it. Don't worry. Just run—no, walk—and tell Mama Pia. And don't eat any pasta before you come to us tomorrow. Leave the rest to me."

Mike reached out a hand. "Thank you, doctor. Thank you very much." He swallowed and added, "Thanks for letting me earn it. That's so important, earning it, on my own."

In eight days Mike Caron was walking with a cane. In two weeks he was behind the wheel of a small but efficient automobile, making the rounds of the properties owned by Doctor Smith, which included small apartment houses, bungalow courts, and single dwellings. Mike worked patiently to solve innumerable problems. He was happy with his leg, and with the job.

Doctor Smith eventually raised his pay, turned the title of the old car over to him, and declared himself completely satisfied with their business deal.

Mike explained to the lunchroom proprietor how he felt about his new work. "This is a great job, you know? I'm learning. Real estate management, it's enjoyable."

Barney said, "The way you talk! Big-shot talk."

"Maybe I'll be a big shot some day. Doc is helping me study the properties from an investment point of view." He dreamed a moment. "I'll buy a couple of pieces for myself. Some day, after I get squared away. I've been thinking of the Valley."

"You owe me four bits," Barney said.

Mike paid him, laughing. "When it happens, the steaks are on me."

He caught sight of Mrs. Desmond one day, driving around, and tried to call her, to tell her he was doing well, but she didn't hear him. He continued to strengthen his leg with isometric exercises.

For weeks Mike climbed ladders to paint houses, ventured upon roofs to repair leaking gutters. He learned about electric wiring. He mixed concrete for a patio. He talked to the tenants and collected rents. Doctor Smith bought another unit and trusted him to hire the help for the project. Mike began to feel important. He was doing something, earning his way. His ego, long injured by failure, blossomed. He banked his money. He had built a small world apart and he was dwelling in it.

Doctor Smith talked with Doctor Westover. "Yes, Mike's fully recovered. To all intents and purposes his hip is as good as new. Not as good as before, you understand, doctor, that couldn't be accomplished. But good enough. However, I am a little worried about him."

"So am I," Doctor Westover said. "He hasn't called my son, you know. Nor any of his former friends."

"That's it. He's built a wall around himself. He believes he is his own master. The world is his oyster. He has no intention of going back to school."

There was a small silence, then Doctor Westover said, "It's always a risk to interfere, isn't it, doctor?"

"Always. But I like the boy."

"Everyone likes him. My son is still worried about him. I'll report the facts as you present them."

"I wish you would. I wish . . . I wish something would happen to jar his complacency." Doctor Smith hung up the phone and sat staring at the wall. Mike was waiting for him in the outer office. The doctor opened the door and admitted him. Mike handed over a batch of rent statements and a bank book.

"Mike, I want to talk to you about that man in the La Brea apartment, Dan Smollett," Doctor Smith began.

"That's what I'm here for. He's behind in his rent. I'll have to ask him to vacate."

"You think so?"

"Well, it's the only way to show a profit on the property. See the expense sheet? The La Brea units eat up the rent with taxes and repairs."

"I'm concerned about Smollett," Doctor Smith said. "He has problems."

"All tenants do," agreed Mike. "But that doesn't give them the right to hedge on the rent. The rent—that's what's important."

"Smollett was once well to do. He became an alcoholic. He went to AA and was cured. I knew him well, in college. Now he's struggling to get a job, any kind of job. He could do what you're doing with ease."

Mike flushed. "What does that mean, doc?"

"A little patience. A little charity, Mike. Think about Smollett. Think about yourself. What's this about not returning to school?"

"I meant to tell you, soon. I like this work. If you'd let me continue I think I could make a go of it."

"Have you talked to your classmates?" He knew the answer, but wanted Mike's reaction.

"Isn't that my business?" Mike's eyes were stony. "Honest, doc, I don't get this."

"You don't seem to catch on to a lot of things, Mike." Doctor Smith sighed. "You've done well. I can't complain. You've carried out the program we agreed upon. I can't force you to go back to school. I won't threaten you with loss of your job. That would be unfair. It's just that I'm worried about you."

"Don't worry about me," said Mike. "I'm fine. I'm eternally grateful to you for letting me earn my way and learn a new business, a new way to live. I'll get along just fine, doc. Thanks for everything."

He breezed out. Doctor Smith sighed, then picked up the telephone again and dialed Doctor Westover.

9

THE EVENING WAS hot and thick with smog. Mike came home, tired but satisfied, greeted Mama Pia, showered, donned slacks and a bright red t-shirt and moccasins. He sat down at the kitchen table, smiling to himself, speaking with the new complete confidence that so worried Mama.

"Hot. Too hot, but I got that fellow Smollett a job. Not much of a job, but a start, driving a truck on a bread route. You know, Helms Bakery, cakes, rolls, pies. Drivers make pretty good money after awhile."

"That's a nice," said Mama Pia. "You see anybody you know?"

"Nope. Haven't time to fool around, you know."

"But you have no friends, Michael."

"Who needs 'em?"

"Ever'body," said she firmly. "Mrs. Katz at the delly, she is a friend. Barney in the beanery is a friend. Me, am I not a friend?"

"You're family," he said affectionately. "That's different. You're my angel of luck. You introduced me to Doctor Smith. I made a deal, everything turned out fine."

"And your college, what about your college?"

"Forget it."

"You mean this is your life? Working and eating and sleeping? This is enough?"

"Good enough for an Italiano boy, Mama. When they took football away, I had to carve out the best life I could."

"They took the football?"

"That's the way it went. Bad luck. But I'm making it. I'm satisfied."

"A boy like you, satisfied?" She shook her head. "No, no is possible. There is a better life for Michael. He must make it for himself, though."

"What's with you tonight, Mama?" He was puzzled. "I don't understand."

"Eat," she said. "Eat the pasta and the meatballs."

He ate with gusto. She moved around, fussing with the pots and pans, the dishes. There was something on her mind, he realized. She was worried about him. He finished his meal and went into the living room and turned on the television. Bob Hope was performing. Perhaps Mama Pia would cheer up if she watched. As he was going to call her the door bell rang. He answered.

Bob Westover said, "Well, amigo, how goes the world?"

Mike fell back, then recovered and said, "Hello, roomie. How did you find me?"

"Can't I come in?"

"Why, sure." Mike indicated the living room. "Mama! Mama Pia. We have company." Confused, he followed Bob into the room, watched Mama enter and go to Bob and take his hand.

"It is good to see you again," she was saying.

"You know each other?" A cloud descended, engulfing Mike. Whatever happened would not be enjoyable, he thought.

"We know each other," Bob said. "You're not as smart as you think you are. It's hard to hide when people want to find you."

"But I'm not ready . . . I mean I didn't want to be found." He floundered.

"Kathy's been worried."

"Kathy's been going with Jimmy Nye," Mike snapped. "It's in the social pages in case you hadn't noticed."

"Did you expect her to go into a convent?"

"I didn't expect anything. I told you that. I told everyone. I'm making it on my own, all by myself. I didn't ask for anything."

Mama Pia cried, "You're quarreling with your friend?"

"No, I'm sorry," Mike said. "Sit down, Bob. Tell me about things."

They sat, but they were not at ease. Bob said, "I

really want to know if you're coming back to school, amigo."

"Not this year. Maybe never. I've paid my doctor, or near enough. But I don't have enough money to go back. Maybe some day I'll finish. I did make up grades last semester, you know."

"I know. We checked."

"You checked. . . ." He broke off. How could he deny their interest in him?

"We knew when you were operated on," Bob was telling him in a matter-of-fact voice. "Kathy called Doctor Smith every hour, made a nuisance of herself."

"What? How did she know about Doctor Smith? How did you find out where I live?"

"We found you through Martin Granger. Mrs. Desmond is concerned about you, also," Bob said. "In spite of the fact her husband is a big USC fan."

"Why can't you all mind your own business?" Mike asked bitterly. "Let me live my own life?"

"But it's not right to be alone," Mama Pia wailed. "Young people, they should be together, enjoy!"

"I can't enjoy if I can't pay."

The door bell rang again. Mama Pia went to attend to it.

"Mike, you've got to think about coming back to school. You know there's no future in this world without a degree. You can continue along the line you've chosen, but get your degree, please!"

"You don't need a degree to . . ." Mike stopped.

Doctor Smith was walking into the room. He said, "Hello, Bob."

"How are you this evening, sir?"

"Just fine." Doctor Smith glanced at Bob, said, "Well, I see you two got together. This was my idea, I want you to know, Mike."

"Your idea?"

"To get Bob over here and talk with you."

"Say, what is this?" Mike's anger was turning his cheeks red, eyes bright. "You're ganging up on me, all of you."

"You might say that."

"And I thought you were my friend. I thought I could trust you!"

"You might say," Doctor Smith went on calmly, "that we ganged up on you from the very beginning. Mama Pia sent you to me. Doctor Westover confirmed my suspicions."

"Doctor Westover? I told them all, I don't want anything for free. I don't want to be obligated!"

"Bob and Kathy were most worried about you and your condition and if you could regain your health and return to school. You're a lucky young man, Mike Caron."

"Yes, you are lucky," Mama Pia said. "Here is this fine boy to ask you to come back to college! How can you refuse to listen to your friends?"

"It's none of their business. None of anyone's business but my own!"

"No man can walk alone," Doctor Smith said.

Bob added, "Mike, everyone needs help at some time or other."

Dimly, Mike knew it was true. But he could not control his emotions. "You're trying to put me into debt. I wanted to live life on my own. You wouldn't let me! You're not my friends!"

Now Bob was angry. "You're accusing wonderful people of mistreating you. That's ridiculous, and you know it."

Mike may have known it, but he couldn't stop. "It's no good, now. I don't want to work for you, Doctor Smith. I don't want handouts from anyone. I'll never go back to school. I . . . I won't stand for interference!"

He dashed out of the room, slamming doors. They could hear him throwing things into a suitcase. In a moment he ran through the hall, and out into the street. They heard his old car start up and drive away.

Mama Pia wept quietly. Doctor Smith went to her and patted her shoulder, saying, "It didn't work very well, did it? I'm sorry."

"Not your fault," she sobbed. "He is sick, that boy. Sick in the head."

"Not so sick," Bob told her. "Just stubborn. And a bit mixed up. I don't know what to make of him. But we'll just have to wait and see what happens, I guess."

"That's right," said Doctor Smith. "Let's wait and see."

They waited a week. There was no sign of Mike,

mainly because he was not staying in one spot. He was moving from place to place in the car, sometimes sleeping in a motel, sometimes on a blanket in the hills.

Mike was experiencing true loneliness. He had only one enemy—himself. After awhile he began to recognize this fact, that he had to beat himself. He did not sleep that night at all, drove aimlessly about the Hollywood hills. A police patrol car stopped him just before dawn.

He showed his license to one of the two patrolmen. He needed a shave and his shirt was soiled. The policeman flashed a light on him, stared with suspicion, then grinned. "Well, it's Mike Caron."

His partner, who was examining the license by the light of the lamps, said, "That's right, Michael Caron."

"The halfback from San Fernando U," said the first cop. "How's it going to be this year, Mike?"

"Oh . . . we'll be in there," said Mike lamely.

"Go on! You ought to go all the way this year. You guys have got the horses. You can go to the Bowl if you get a few breaks."

"Oh, I don't know about that." Mike felt like an outcast, a liar. Why didn't he say right out that he wasn't going back?

"Worrying about it? Driving around, trying to shake the shakes?" asked the policeman sympathetically. "Guess you'll be registering tomorrow."

"Uh . . ." Mike sat up straight. "You're right. We do have a chance. My leg's a lot better."

"Can you make that cut?"

"No. I'll never make that cut again."

"Oh, that's too bad!"

"We've got Danning, you know. I'll make myself useful, one way or another."

"Big Westover goes both ways. He's a dandy," said the policeman. "I live in the valley, you know. I see every game I can get to."

"Yes, we've got a chance, all right," Mike said. His mind was no longer whirling. "Guess I'll run along home, now."

"Take it easy, Mike," said the officer, taking the license from his indifferent companion and returning it. "And good luck."

Mike drove back to the city but did not return to Mama Pia's house. The next morning he was dozing in the back seat of his car when Doctor Smith pulled into the garage beneath his office.

"Good morning, doc," Mike called.

"Well. Good morning, Mike. You look slightly beat. Better come up and have coffee."

"No, I won't take a minute. Had to see you quick as I could."

"That's fine."

"Wanted to tell you. That fellow, that Mr. Smollett. He'd do a good job for you."

"You don't want to come back to work?"

"No. I've decided to take an exam for a small scholarship."

"Oh! I see."

"Maybe I could help Smollett week ends, sometimes.

I figure I'll stay with Mama Pia. I saved enough to pay the rent for awhile. If Smollett doesn't agree I'll make out, find something to do."

"I'm sure he will." The doctor carefully did not show elation, spoke in a matter-of-fact tone. "You've hit on some good ideas."

"Well, Smollett's a fine man. Driving a truck, that's not right for him."

"I agree."

They were silent for a moment, then Mike managed a weak grin. "It's hard for me to admit when I'm wrong. But I'm saying it, now. You did everything for me that anyone could do, and there I went, acting like the king of the road."

"Everyone has to find his way, Mike."

"Well, thanks for steering me right. I'll never forget it, not ever."

"I believe you."

"Have to get a bit of rest, then register. They'll let me take the exam, I know they will."

"Well, Mike. Good luck."

"Well, thanks again." He stuck out his hand. They shook, hard, and Mike drove out of the garage and back toward Mama Pia's. He scooped up the newspaper from the porch before entering the house. It flipped open to the society section. A headline hit him right between the eyes.

Miss Kathy Nelson was engaged to be married to James Nye, USC football star.

10

KATHY NELSON AND Bob Westover came down the hall, noting a familiar figure at the bulletin board, copying down schedule information. Kathy clutched Bob's arm and said, "There he is."

"Doggone if it ain't," Bob drawled.

"He won the scholarship, then?"

"Yes. He took a special exam. To let them see what he had or hadn't forgotten. He did okay."

"Aren't you going to speak to him?" she demanded.

"I'm waiting."

"For what?"

"Just waiting," Bob said evasively. "Are you going to the cafeteria? I have to meet Nancy."

"I'm going to speak to him."

"Be my guest," Bob said. "But you are engaged to another man, in case you've forgotten."

"I didn't say I was going to marry Mike!"

"That's right. You didn't. But you are going to run right straight to him, aren't you?"

Mike folded his notebook and turned away from the bulletin board. Kathy made a beeline toward him. Bob scratched his head and headed toward the cafeteria.

Kathy extended her hands to Mike. "It's wonderful to see you back in school."

He was evidently prepared for her. He took her left hand in his, glanced down at the third finger and said, "Congratulations, Kathy."

"You congratulate the groom, not the bride," she told him, trying to smile brightly. "You wish me the best."

"Best wishes."

They stared at one another for a moment. Neither of them was at ease. Both were trying to carry off the meeting without injuring the other.

"I acted like a real jerk last time I saw you," he apologized. "I've learned better, I hope."

"Forget it. You've put on weight, haven't you?"

"About twenty pounds. Doctor Smith prescribed some exercises. I've been working for him, you know."

"It's . . . becoming. I mean . . . you look well."

"I'm fine. But you seem to have lost a little weight. Haven't you?"

"Not much." She bit her lip. She'd lost eight pounds. "Where are you staying?"

"Mama Pia's, where else? The old heap buzzes the freeways like a veteran should. Few minutes extra each day but the price is right and I love Mama Pia."

"It sounds fine," she said.

"How's Jimmy doing at USC?" He kept his voice steady.

"Oh, fine. Football as usual. You know Jimmy. Same character."

"I bet."

Kathy's cheeks burned as he regarded her in the moment of silence that followed. Then she said, "Well, Nancy and Bob are waiting for me in the eatery. Won't you join us?"

"No, thanks. 'I'm busier than a cat on a hot tin shanty," he said, pleasantly enough. "See you around, Kathy. Lots of luck."

He walked away with no trace of a limp. She watched until he turned a corner in the direction of the athletic department, then put a hand to her cheek, dropped it, stared at the dampness thereon, her eyes blurred. Then she went out of doors to her car. She drove off campus alone, her mind fighting for control of mixed emotions.

It was a clear day in the San Fernando Valley. Mike Caron was wearing a new number but he had been given a Varsity jersey, a concession he had not expected. He heard his name called in stentorian accents.

"Caron!"

Mike looked up, aware of all the eyes on him. He could distinguish Bob Westover, tall among the linemen. He signified, by waving, that he had heard.

"Report to Dillon."

Mike hunted for Knox Dillon, a former pro all-star who was this season coaching the line. Dillon wasn't hard to find. He stared hard at Mike. "You put on some lard."

"Twenty pounds," Mike admitted.

"You're too little for a tackle."

"I know."

"Can you run at all?"

"Try me."

"Oh, we'll try you. We'll try you, boy. You had any body contact?"

"I'm ready for scrimmage."

"You got a big opinion of you," Dillon observed. "There's Pascal and Sigurd and four big sophs ahead of you. Randolph insisted on you wearing that jersey. I dunno."

"I'd be rusty on offense. Want to try me at linebacker?"

"I got Killeen, Osmanski, Gould. I got kids behind them like oxen."

"I don't expect to star," Mike told him. "Get it straight, Dillon. I'm here to help if I can. You're boss. I'm not arguing with you. Whatever you say is all right with me."

"Thanks," said the big coach with heavy sarcasm. "I sure appreciate it."

"I'm not being smart, or funny, either." Mike spoke evenly, forcing himself to grin. Dillon rubbed him the

111

wrong way but Mike had a mission to perform and meant to pull it through.

"Okay. Go work out with defense. But follow the offense around for a couple days. You'll do better on offense . . . if you make it at all."

Mike nodded and trotted off. He knew that everyone, especially Bob Westover, was watching him curiously. He joined the defensive squad. Asher Brown came over and held out his hand.

"Welcome, pal," said the big Negro end.

"Hi, Brownie. I'm back where I belong," Mike said.

"You belong," agreed Brown. "If it's football, you belong."

The others seemed agreeable if not so cordial. They worked out on machines built to withstand their butting and grunting and tackling. It was hard labor, but Mike had been doing hard labor all summer long. He learned a lot, he thought, from Brown and from Sandy Gould, the senior middlebacker.

Westover was working with both offense and defense again this year, Mike noted. The captain was also an invaluable bulwark of the weak bench. Mike's job might be to free a guard to spell Bob some of the time.

They came face to face at last. For a moment neither spoke, then Mike said, "Well, here we are again."

"Glad to see you," said Bob, his tone cool.

"Thought I'd have a look at how the other half lives."

112

"We can use bench. Are you sure you're all right to play?"

"They say so. They tell me I'm dumb but strong."

"Hope you make it." Bob turned away toward the offense lining up for scrimmage. Mike kept on the outskirts as the defense, under Asher Brown, organized itself to meet the first-team's attack.

Dan Kyle, the brilliant quarterback, paused, adjusting his headguard and said, "Mike, glad to see you."

"How are you, Dan?"

"Old and weary. But we'll be in there. Wish you were running again."

"Danning will do all right."

Kyle gave him a worried look. "Will he?"

"Sure, he'll break in and be okay."

"I still wish you were handling it."

Kyle took charge. To settle down the offensive formation, he called for a quick handoff to Tug Manning, the tank-sized fullback. Asher Brown foresaw the design and charged. The front four pinched in and Tug got only a yard. Mike moved uneasily, noting that the linebackers had been a bit slow.

On the next try Kyle retreated, pitched out to Danning. The hard-running back cut on a dime and punched past Brown for five. Again the linebackers, Killeen and Osmanski, were slow in backing up. Evidently they had not yet adjusted to scrimmage. Players could get stale during the summer.

Dillon came in, breathing fire, shouting. Brown

113

shook his head and huddled the defense. Dillon continued to yell.

Kyle faked a handoff and passed sharply down and out to the side lines. Morgan, the lanky, durable Kentuckian, reached and took the pass and stepped out of bounds for the first down.

Dillon fired, "You're too slow in there! Move a little!"

Randolph refrained from comment, remaining on his movable tower, watching. Mike walked to where he could watch the guards on offense, noting that they had achieved excellent timing, and were working like a team of trained horses, belting over the defense, opening holes for the runners.

Kyle again sent Tug reeling into the line. Brown and Tillou and Miller and Ambrose crushed the attempt. On second down Danning faked, went deep. Kyle arched a long one. Danning got behind Homeier, grabbed the ball, and ran for the first touchdown of the season.

Dillon spun in rage and bumped into Mike. "Get in there at the middlebacker," he roared. "I want to have a talk with Gould. Let's see what you can do."

Mike readied his headguard as they brought the ball back to the offense unit's twenty to put it into play. More experienced linemen should have been spelling Sandy. Dillon had a right to try him out, though, before the opening game with Michigan.

"Sandy's rusty. Got a muscle pull, too. You know

their patterns, just stick your head in where you think they're going," Brown advised.

It was a test Mike welcomed. He stood behind the poised big four up front and watched Kyle. He knew that the canny quarterback would be ready to cross him up, but he also knew that the offense was still a bit creaky, as always in the first scrimmages.

Kyle called them to the line for what looked like the usual line plunge. Mike dropped off. The guards pulled back. Mike was certain the quarterback was pulling a first-down pass.

Then, too late, he saw that Tug was getting it on the draw play, a delayed sortie through the tackle. Mike should have been there. He tried to get there.

He was a split second too late. Tug rambled past him and up the middle for ten yards before Homeier and Hunter ganged up on the burly fullback.

Dillon was hollering. Gould was putting his head-guard on again. In the huddle Brown said, "Burned you, Mike. He's that way, the rascal."

"Fooled me," admitted Mike. "Glad he's on our side."

Kyle had them aligned again. He again retreated, but now he pitched out to Danning.

This time Mike found his legs and with a burst of his old speed traveled on the angle of Danning's rush. He saw the high knees and launched himself, flying through the air, taking Danning about the middle, spinning and swinging the halfback. The result was a spectacular roll on the sward, with Danning fighting to get free long past the whistle blown by Mike Tilden, acting referee.

Mike broke loose and said, "Easy does it, Danning."

"Don't you try to show me up," growled the new running back.

"Easy," Mike repeated. He had tossed the play for a loss. "You're a hero already, don't spoil it."

Danning glared at him, went back to the huddle. Mike saw Gould coming in and removed his head-guard. He walked to the side lines. Dillon greeted him with a scowl.

"You don't have to kill them, just stop 'em."

"You want me to hit him low? He'd run me over." Mike tried to take off the sting with a grin he found hard to manage. It wasn't simple, trying to get along with everyone, he thought. It was going to be a long, hard season.

Dillon said grudgingly, "You did okay, Caron. We'll be using you some, when you catch onto the system."

"Thanks, coach," said Mike, meaning it. A soft answer turneth away wrath, he thought.

Randolph was giving an order. "Caron . . . follow the offense."

It was, Mike corrected, going to be a long, hard opening day of practice. They were probing him, trying to find his place in the scheme of big-time football. There was no margin for error. He shifted his attention to the offense.

Randolph was always looking for men who could go

both ways on occasion. The SFU bench was never as strong as UCLA's or USC's. The head coach knew his business. None complained, especially those with an eye on professional football. Mike knew he would never make it in the pro's. He would be giving his all for SFU, not for future money.

Randolph had insisted that all players on offense learn all other assignments. Mike had not been a top student and now had to think back and think hard as he watched the play proceed. He found that he could recall some of the basics, some of the plays, but not all of them.

He kept his eye on Sigurd and Pascal, the guards, both strong and quick. He admired the way Bob Westover dominated the line, watching everything, always alert, the perfect athlete, the typical team captain. He was too absorbed to note that Randolph had climbed down from his tower and was walking beside him. The head coach spoke.

"Mike."

"Uh, yes, sir."

"Timing is the most important factor in offensive line play. Count the split seconds. You have to know the quarterback's cadence."

"Yes, sir."

"I want to try you, but don't get worried. I liked the way you moved, considering the extra weight you're carrying. You took Danning down the right way."

"He's a hard man to pull down single-o."

"I know." The coach was watching the guards pull back to defend Kyle on a pass formation. "Can you remember enough of the system to give it a try?"

Mike said, "You want to see if I can pull and make the cut?"

"Go in for Sigurd. Listen to Kyle's count. Hold steady until the snap . . . oh, go ahead in there!"

Mike again donned the headguard, snapped the chin strap. Westover looked at him quizzically as he reported. Pascal grinned, showing a gap where two teeth had been lost to USC in last year's battle and said, "Welcome to the foot sloggers, Caron."

The linemen had no reason to love him, Mike knew. He had not been kind to them in the past. He decided to keep his mouth shut and take what came.

Kyle called for a pitchout to Danning. This would force Mike to retreat, spin, and lead interference. It was a maneuver only the best and swiftest guards could manage with grace. He doubted his ability as he lined up in the three-point stance and listened to signals.

Foran bent over the ball. Mike was facing the front four, the monsters of defense, now. If he made a wrong move they would crunch him like a paper cup and throw him aside.

The ball was snapped. Mike wheeled. His leg held. He was not as strong and quick as before, but he got out there. He knew Danning, behind him, was looking for the blocks. He hunched his shoulders and dived against Asher Brown.

The collision was stunning. Mike saw stars. He felt as if a truck had run over him.

Brown did not make the tackle. But Sandy Gould, diagnosing the play, grabbed Danning and held him until Killeen could swamp him for a loss. Mike got groggily to his feet amid Danning's shrill, loud cries. "Dumbbell! Clown! Why can't you take 'em out? How can a guy run with no blockin'?"

Mike found himself looking into Bob Westover's eyes. The captain was regarding him without expression. Mike lifted one shoulder pad, said quietly, "Well, here's where we came in."

11

MAMA PIA SAID, "Football! Hitting and grabbing and kicking. No, I tell you. I don't want to go."

"But I have a ticket for you. Opening game will be very exciting. I probably won't play much, but you'd enjoy seeing the people, the bands, everything," Mike pleaded.

"I'd enjoy? People hurting?"

"Mama, they wear lots of padding. I showed you, I brought some home just to show you."

She prodded him in the middle with a stiff finger and he winced. "You got padding there? Ha?"

"Mama, it doesn't hurt. We're all trained for it."

"You should live through today, September twenty-three, a lovely sunshiny day." She rolled her eyes to the ceiling.

"Mama, I should think you'd be proud that I'm playing."

"You might not play, you say. So . . . why should I go?"

"I give up," said Mike. "Here, take two tickets. Give one to Barney or somebody. Every week I am going to bring you two tickets, you can do what you want with 'em." He hugged her, slipped the pasteboards into her hand, and ran for the door.

She called after him, "I light a candle, you don't get killed! Football!"

As the door closed behind him she turned to the radio in the sitting room and tuned in the valley station, KGIL, which carried all the SFU football games. She would not switch stations for the rest of the day . . . until she knew Mike was safe. If he happened to be put into the game she'd be scared. But she wouldn't miss it for the world.

Mike kept on the Hollywood Freeway with his old but faithful car till he hit the Ventura Freeway intersection. From there it was fifteen miles to the SFU turnoff. That led to the road that led directly to the field house. Michigan rarely came to California for opening game so there was much activity even this early. Bands were tootling and cheerleaders were warming up. Mike parked and walked into the dressing room.

Only Coach Randolph and Bob Westover were present. They stopped talking as he entered.

"Go right ahead," Mike commented curtly. "Funny how the guy you're talking about will walk in so often, isn't it?"

121

Randolph said guiltily, "Nothing against you, Mike. You've taken hold . . . well, I've never seen anyone learn so fast. But we think you're best at defense."

"I think so, too," said Mike. "Danning can't tangle with me if I'm on the other unit."

"Danning has no more rights on this team than you," Bob Westover spoke. He kept his voice impersonal. Though he had gone all out to find Mike the other's behavior on that occasion had cooled his warmth. Mike hadn't moved to resume their intimacy either, for reasons of pride.

"A star running back thinks he's pretty special," Mike reminded them. "I used to feel the same way." He went to his corner cubicle. It was not easy for him to maintain good humor, to accept everything that came his way without striking back, except in humorous accents.

Danning was hardest to take. The loud-mouth back felt that he was a star, that the success of the team depended upon him. He looked at Mike with a gleam in his eye, smug because he had inherited the first-team job without having to work for it.

This attitude could not be good for the team. Mike was thinking more about the team nowadays. He figured Doc Smith had had something to do with that. Only that morning his mentor had said, "Nothing is worth doing if it is for your own benefit only."

Mike had never thought along those lines. He could not tell anyone of his change of heart. Who would believe him? He dressed with care and walked outside.

Randolph gave the squad last-moment instructions before all forty-five trotted out on the field in their green and white jerseys and gold pants.

Michigan's band was marching off the field amidst great beating of drums. Forty thousand people, with more to arrive later, were jamming the stadium.

Bob Westover and Asher Brown went out to meet the visiting captains, quarterback Fran Close and linebacker Hobie Barker. Michigan won the coin toss and elected to receive. Randolph, already nervous, chewing on a toothpick, came to Mike, saying, "You know what to do. Straight down and clear the blockers."

Mike said, "Yes, sir."

"Got to get the ball. That Close can pass."

"Yes, sir." Mike, because of his experience, was on the special team, the squad that went down under kicks, performing dirty jobs anonymously. They were not on the field long enough for anyone to remember their numbers. Not that the fans ever cheered for guards anyway, Mike added to himself, without rancor.

He ran to his position in the middle of the thin line as Bob Westover teed up the ball. Mike, too precious to risk, had never been in this line-up before. Danning was on the bench now, waiting for SFU to get possession of the ball. So were the other stars of offense.

Mike, butterflies in his belly, palms sweating, waited for the kickoff. He bent his knees, flexed his arms, watched Westover. The referee poised his whistle.

In the stands Kathy Nelson sat with Nancy Waite and two classmates. None of the friends spoke of Mike. Kathy's eyes, though, were glued on her former boy friend, number 49.

Doctor Ransom Smith, conscious of strain also, sat in his accustomed reserved seat. He, too, was watching number 49.

The radio announcer was droning names and numbers, referring to the group afield as "the suicide squad," and going on to comment, "Mike Caron, former running star, is now a guard wearing number forty-nine. Can SFU carry on without this brilliant backfielder? . . . There is the whistle!"

Mama Pia, at home, voiced a prayer.

Mike Caron ran step for step with Westover, heard rather than saw, contact of toe and ball. He aimed himself at the vanguard of blockers downfield, who were forming a line against the Michigan receiver, a swift runner. Mike hurled himself beneath the feet of one giant in maize and blue and rolled through. When the man crashed down, Mike launched a block at a second. An SFU tackle slashed in and dropped the receiver on the nineteen-yard line.

Mike, unheralded and unnoticed, trotted off the field. On the bench he applied himself to watching line play, forcing his attention away from the ball and the men who tried to advance it by run or pass. The men of defense did not talk with him. He was not yet one of them. This was, he knew, something he had to accept. He could not demand from anyone, he had only to do his job.

Mike would play, but not start. He would probably log enough time to earn a letter. And he would be, Randolph had told him, a welcome adjunct to the team. This was not terribly inspiring, but it was what Mike wanted. He had only to remain in the background, allow insults to roll off, control his ego . . . and play hard in an unfamiliar position.

The Michigans lunged at the SFU defense. Fran Close was a superb performer. On the first play he faked a handoff, dropped back into the cup, and tossed a soft side lines pass to Gore, a tall, quick end, for eleven yards. On the second play he rolled out, forced Homeier back by feigning a throw, then ran for another first down on the forty-five.

Randolph said, "Caron!"

Mike couldn't believe his ears. "Yes, sir?"

"Go in and tell them to rush that passer, right now!"

Mike grabbed his helmet and sped to the huddle. "Coach says to red dog."

"Well, okay," agreed Asher Brown. "But red dogging's dangerous so early, against this character."

Mike was to back up the SFU line, jitterbug through a spot in the Michigan line, with intent to commit mayhem on Fran Close. The Big Ten quarterback, eyes shifting, stood behind his center, uttering numbers. Mike sensed disaster as the ball was snapped.

He followed orders, slammed through at Close. A

guard, retreating, hit him, hit him again with folded forearms, hit him a third time. Asher Brown went past this man with upflung arms. Tillou and Miller did the same while Ambrose got himself upset in a pinch.

Close laughed in their faces, flipping a short one to Franciosa, his fullback, who was led by half the Michigan team as he fled down the side lines. Mike wheeled and followed. Danzig, the SFU free safety, finally slowed down the runner and the blockers. Mike was able to grab Franciosa from behind and down him on the ten-yard marker.

Sandy Gould replaced, muttered to Mike, "The coach blew that one, all right. Nice pursuit, Mike."

On the side lines Randolph was talking to Bob Westover. "Go in for Ambrose, they're dumping him. Try and get that ball!"

Westover galloped onto the field. Randolph ignored Mike. One of the subs, though, said, "You sure kept after 'em, Caron."

Mike watched Fran Close fake out SFU. He slid over on a bootleg rollout to score. Then the Michigan quarterback kicked the extra point to make it 7 for the visitors, 0 for the home team. Mike returned to block for the receiver on the kick reception.

Fran Close also kicked off. Mike wondered if he handled the water bucket in his spare time. The ball went up and soared over the goal posts and out of play. Mike trotted back to the bench.

Dillon was waiting for him. "If you were stronger,

you could of turned that guard on that red dog. You're supposed to get past him, not through him."

"Yes, sir," Mike agreed.

"Next time go around him."

"I'll try, sir," said Mike. He was beginning to feel like a robot, emptily repeating vapidities. There had been no way around the Michigan guard. The traffic had been too thick. Couldn't Dillon see that Close had figured it all out, called an audible at the line designed to sucker the red dog? On the bench Mike turned his attention to Sigurd's play.

Dan Kyle did not intend to be outshone in the gambling and imagination departments. From the SFU twenty, on first down, the quarterback threw to Danning. Westover tore down a linebacker, while Danning got loose and went to midfield.

On the next play Kyle, with even better protection, tincanned around, uncorked a bomb. It flew high and far. Morgan, the swifter end, caught it on the ten. He straight-armed one opponent and eluded the other. Westover kicked the extra point to tie the game. Randolph congratulated the offense as the men came off the field.

Mike went on as Westover teed up the ball. It was beginning to look like a put and take game, Mike thought. Neither defense had shown anything yet.

The kick was not very deep, but it was also not very high, which gave Michigan little time to form blocking for the ball carrier. Mike's speed took him down there.

The kicker, Westover, anxious to overcome possible error, was not far behind. When the receiver caught the ball, Mike hit him midship with all his might. The Michigan runner went one way. The ball went another.

Westover fell on the ball.

Mike got up and ran off the field. All he could hear was the name of the man who had recovered—Westover.

"Nice going, Mike," Asher Brown complimented. "That's the way to hit."

"It hurts," Mike answered, rubbing a bruised arm.

"Sure, it hurts. But how do you think the other guy feels?"

They laughed, waiting for Kyle to produce a touchdown. They waited and waited. Michigan had suddenly come to life on defense. Westover went in and attempted a field goal. It was wide to the right and the score remained tied.

Michigan came confidently back to the attack. Sandy Gould broke through and dropped Close on his own twelve-yard line before he could pass. A run failed. A long pass was almost intercepted by Danzig. Michigan punted.

That's how the game went throughout the remainder of the half. Instead of a wide-open scoring contest it had become a triumph for defense. Mike did not see action again before they went to the dressing room between the second and third periods.

Randolph had the blackboard ready. He lectured furiously, while Hodges, the trainer, and his aides worked on various injuries, scratches, and abrasions. Mike, sitting alone in a corner, listened intently.

"We can win this game," was Randolph's final pronouncement. "We've got to win it if we're going to have the season we deserve."

Asher Brown murmured, "He says 'we' like he's out there getting hit by those monsters." This good-natured comment did not require an answer.

Mike filed back to the war at the procession's tail. SFU's touchdown had been tinged with luck, coming after the fumble, he thought. The home team was not inspired. Even Westover seemed unable to drum up the dedication needed to take this game from Michigan.

SFU's turn came to receive. Fran Close kicked it deep. Mike was in the vanguard of the blockers as Danning caught the ball on the two and began running it back. Mike rammed a shoulder into a big Michigan lineman. At that moment Danning, not looking where he was going, made a cut to avoid another enemy, and ran into Mike's back. A third man yanked him down on the twenty. He came up glaring.

"What's with you, Caron? Can't you even get outa my way?"

"Nope," Mike said. "I'm just a broke-down old wagon."

He went off, leaving Danning staring after him. It's better not to argue, Mike told himself. Maybe he was building up a head of steam that would blow a hole in the scenery. Meantime, he was holding it all inside and following the course of the game.

129

Dan Kyle's passes having failed to click, Randolph had ordered a running game. Danning took it on the first play for five yards. Tug Manning got four. Kyle himself plunged over a guard for the first down.

Michigan moved in. Dan threw a little down-and-outer to Danning, who broke over midfield before he was tackled. Randolph began to snap his fingers in anticipation. SFU was rolling.

Again Danning ran, this time off tackle, for eight. Mike found himself on the side lines, kneeling, squinting. Danning hit the other side for five, taking two men with him. Sigurd and Pascal were hitting low enough to hoist the bigger Michigans up and out of play for a split second. Danning was cutting into the hole with the sure stride and fine eye of a real star.

Kyle faked to Danning and went back, then slipped the ball to Tug on a draw play. The hole up the middle was enormous. The fullback rumbled to the Michigan fifteen-yard line.

Randolph called, "Caron."

Mike went to him, adjusting the chin strap of his helmet.

"Tell Kyle to use Danning."

"Yes, sir."

Mike raced on to the field and tapped a resentful Sigurd. He gave the message to Kyle, then crouched in position like a coiled spring. Kyle counted off, the ball went back.

Mike hit the man opposite him and drove. Westover hammered his man into the pair of them. The hole was there.

Danning cannonballed into it. He brushed right past the middle linebacker. Michigan had been looking for something fancy. Three men fell on Mike, one kicking him in the jaw. Danning scored.

Mike was aching on the side lines when Westover converted, to make it SFU 14, Michigan 7. Westover had hurt Mike as much as the opposition. His cheek was bleeding. Trainer Hodges was attending to Danning's jersey, which had been torn afield.

"Are you all right?" Bob Westover asked, peering at Mike. He was taking a rest as fresh defensive men went on and Dan Kyle lined up the kick, a sometimes Randolph strategy.

"Nope," said Mike. "But I'll live."

"That was a lovely charge you made, in there."

"I was all right until you kicked me."

"That was a Michigan man." Westover grinned. "Same old Mike, aren't you?"

"I'm afraid not," Mike answered. He was smiling, but his tone was cool. He was not ready to resume relations with Westover and friends. Pride.

"Well. . . ." Bob seemed a bit hurt. "Get Hodges to attend to that cut. We don't want infections."

"I can wait. I'm learning about waiting." Mike turned to one of the assistants, who wiped the blood from his face and applied an astringent and a piece of tape. He was far from weary, but this was altogether different from playing in the backfield. He caught Brown's eye and big Asher winked merrily. Where would they be without us? the wink conveyed.

The game went back to humdrum tactics, feinting, fencing between the two good quarterbacks. Mike went in and out a couple of times with nothing much important taking place. Then came the final five minutes of the game.

Michigan received a kick on their fifteen and ran it back to the thirty. Fran Close exploded again. He passed for a first down at midfield.

Randolph moved uneasily, sent in orders to use the umbrella defense against the long pass. Close responded by running the ball three times in succession. He garnered another first down on the thirty. Two more plays and he brought Michigan to the fifteen, again with brilliant running and blocking by Levy and Jones, the guards. The referee stopped proceedings to announce that only two minutes were left in the game. Michigan had three time-outs left, though. Mike knew what this meant. A score and a two-point conversion and SFU would have no time for a comeback.

Randolph was talking with Dillon. Michigan went into the middle of the line and got four yards to the eleven. Randolph croaked, "Caron!"

Mike buckled on his headguard. Randolph, kneeling, fists clenched, did not look at him.

"Tell Brown to tighten up. Tell him . . . Oh, tell him to knock down that quarterback!"

132

"Yes, sir!" Mike shot onto the field. "Coach says to knock down Close."

"Yeah," Brown said. The big Negro's eyes were narrowed, humorlessly. "We've been trying. That front line keeps getting tougher."

Then they were waiting for the attack and Mike was roaming behind center, trying to remember everything he had learned as an offensive player, trying to read Close's mind. He guessed a pass but was far from confident.

The ball was snapped. Mike started for the hole, then saw Levy pull back from his guard position.

Mike leaped backward. Ostrowski had come through without the ball. Mike ran and jumped and put up his hand. The ball, thrown on a line, glanced off his wrist. He spun to follow its course. Asher Brown was already there.

The big tackle nipped it out of the air. He carried it in one huge paw, running toward the Michigan goal, with nobody in front. Mike belted out Close as he tried to follow, picked himself up and ran, saw a Michigan catch the lumbering defensive end from behind on the SFU thirty-yard line.

The offense, Sigurd among them, returned to the field, and Mike went back to the bench. Dillon was regarding him peculiarly. Randolph asked, "Was it you that deflected that ball?"

"Sort of," Mike told him. Asher Brown, sweating and grinning, interposed. "This Mike, he's either great or lucky. He broke it open twice today."

133

Randolph said, "Humph."

Dillon began uncertainly, "I've seen lucky players before."

"I'm a beginner," Mike explained. "You've heard of that kind, surely. Beginner's luck."

He headed for the lockers. He was bleeding again. No one commented on his going. The game was over to all intents and purposes.

Mike looked at himself in a mirror. The face guard hadn't protected him much. "Hello, lineman," he greeted his image. "How do you like being a second-string lineman?" He saluted and answered himself, "I don't like it a whole lot . . . but it's better than not being in the game."

He was still in the showers when the team came in whooping and happy at having made such a good start on a tough season. Nobody but Asher Brown paid much attention to him. The big end, speaking lightly, gave Mike to understand that he had appreciated what Mike had done that day.

"It's okay, Ash. Thanks."

Next they were talking about making ends meet. Brown asked diffidently, "You need anything, Mike? Like a little job?"

"You bet I do."

"Well . . . a couple of us got a little thing going. We're baby-sitters."

Mike laughed.

Asher said, "It's a way to make a nice, easy dollar and you can study at the same time."

"Are second-stringers acceptable?"

"Sure. You can work tonight. People want to celebrate. Okay?"

"Okay? Perfect!"

He didn't have a girl to celebrate with, so he might as well make some money.

12

BOB WESTOVER AND Nancy, Jimmy Nye and Kathy were at The Grove. Bobo was with another party. She kept knifing Kathy with glances, but Kathy didn't notice. She wasn't noticing anybody.

Jimmy complained, "Youall won the game, why so glum?"

"Oh, I'm all right," she said.

"I flew in from San Francisco just to be with you," he persisted. "We won, too, you know."

"I'm very happy for all of us," she said.

"Then let's dance." He led her onto the floor.

Bobo danced with a lanky USC man. She called, "How lucky we are. Some people are working. Kathy's old boy friend, for instance, is baby-sitting my cousin's baby."

Jimmy swung Kathy away, flushing, muttering, "She never gives up. What did I ever see in her?"

"Oh, Bobo's fun," Kathy said. "When I don't have a headache."

"You have a lot of headaches lately," Jimmy complained.

Kathy said weakly, "Now, Jimmy."

"You haven't been well for weeks, baby. Weeks. Ever since Mike-boy returned to good old SFU. You're starting to give me a headache."

"Well, why don't you dance with Bobo, then?"

"Maybe I will. Come to think of it, I always had a pretty good time with Bobo. She's not a pill."

"Well, take this with you." Kathy stopped dancing and pulled at her finger. She deposited his ring in his hand. He glared at her.

"You can tell Mike Caron I'll see him on November twenty-seventh. He'd better keep his eyes open that afternoon."

"Oh, go spin your top," Kathy said. Her eyes were bright. Her headache had vanished. She returned to Bob and Nancy. "Shall we leave? Jimmy and I just broke up. I haven't felt better in weeks!"

"Let me pay for this and we'll evaporate."

In the car the three of them talked about Mike Caron. Bob told them how he had performed that afternoon, about the things they could not see from the stands. "He worked hard for no credit. He's changed. Here we sit, the three of us," Bob said. "And once again we're talking about Mike Caron. It's a passing strange thing."

137

"He does that to you," Kathy told them softly. "There's something about him. He does it to you."

Mike tiptoed into the luxurious nursery and looked at the little boy. The little boy looked back at him.

"Hi," said Mike.

"Hi," said the boy, who was eight.

"Can't sleep?"

"I was dreamin'."

"But you're not scared?"

"Nope."

"Then will you go asleep again?"

"Oh, sure." The boy grinned at him. "You're the football player, ain't you?"

"Aren't I, you mean?"

"Aren't you?"

"Yes, I'm the football player."

"My papa says you're a hardhead. Is that good or bad?"

Mike looked down at the book in his hand. He sighed and answered, "Your papa is right. It's not so good. Did he tell you how not to be a hardhead?"

"I don't think papa knows."

"Well, thanks anyway," Mike said. "Sleep, now?"

"Okay," said the boy. "Hope you win all your games."

Mike returned to the den and sank into a deep leather chair. He could no longer concentrate on the textbook. He wondered what Kathy and Jimmy Nye were doing. He wondered about Nancy and Bob. He wondered why he could not walk up to them and be friendly and have things the way they were before.

He could not find the answer. Nothing was simple any more.

The SFU team went north and beat Stanford, but not by as large a margin as had USC. Oregon State visited on October 8th and SFU ran over them, 26–0. Mike saw a lot of action in that one, due to Sigurd's pulled muscle.

They played Washington there, had a close one, 21 to 14.

The UCLA game was crucial. SFU squeaked it out in the closing moments of the thrilling game. California at Berkeley was easy. The clash between SFU and Notre Dame was heard across the country. Mike played both offense and defense. Although he was getting more and more time afield as the season wore on, little was said about him. Each time he performed he was smothered in anonymity. However, one or two of the sports writers were beginning to get the idea.

Notre Dame had a fantastic passing combination, a quarterback and end, both swift and elusive. Mike on the blitz chased the passer all afternoon and in the last quarter with the score tied, caught him on the Notre Dame thirty.

Knowing the boy was inexperienced, knowing Asher Brown was somewhere near, Mike wrenched apart the ND quarterback's arms, a legal move. Asher reached out and took away the ball.

Dan Kyle calmly threw two passes, the final one to Morgan, who had become his prime target. SFU scored, to the beating of drums.

USC had done equally well, defeating Notre Dame at South Bend, an almost impossible feat. Everyone began looking to the contest of November 27th as the game to decide the national championship. The pressure became terrific.

Joe Danning had done all that was asked of him all season. Experts mentioned him for All America. He was a running fool, they said. No one man could bring him down. He climbed into the holes quicker than Mike Caron ever had.

A wire-service sports writer in Texas first perceived who, since Sigurd had slowed down and was playing only half the time, was opening many of the holes for Danning. He did a stirring story on Mike Caron, explaining how last year's running back, now playing on the line, was breaking Danning loose for many of his advances.

Danning was furious. He voiced his objections in the locker room before the Ohio State game. Mike was in his corner carefully taping his leg.

"Some lousy story," Danning complained loudly. "Some cornball story. All linemen are great. Backs only have to run through the holes. What about the times they louse up and don't open a hole and we gain four or five?"

140

"It never happens," Asher Brown told him.

"Oh, you guys on defense are different. You're great," Danning conceded. "It's the bums on offense that get me down. If they gave me running room half the time, we'd swamp everybody we meet."

Westover said sharply, "That's enough of that, Danning. You may be kidding, but it's not funny."

"Who's kidding?" came the loud voice. "Did you see Caron miss that block in Texas? Nailed me for a loss."

"I'm not interested. I'm telling you to shut up!" Westover, suddenly furious, loomed over the halfback.

"You can't shut me up. It's a free country. You're not my boss."

Westover said, "Never mind the boss bit. You shut up or I'll clobber you into the next county!"

Coach Randolph came running from his office, where he had been able to overhear the exchange. "That'll be enough from both of you! Get dressed and get on that field."

For a moment it seemed as if Westover would pick up coach and player and bang their heads together. Then he exhaled slowly and pointedly. His voice grew smooth and calm. "Yes, sir. You're right." White-faced, shaking, he crossed to his locker, facing Mike's corner. Mike wagged his head, held up thumb and fore-finger in the 'okay' signal.

Color returned as Bob managed a wry grin.

Mike drifted over to him. "You told him, cap'n."

"I could've murdered him."

"No, you couldn't. Wouldn't blame you for trying. But we've got two games to play. Line starts fighting the backfield, what happens?"

Bob said, "You kept your cool all right, Mike. Thanks."

Mike shrugged. "Shall we see what we can do with the Ohios?"

The team from Columbus was not the powerhouse of past seasons. It had courage and strength, as always, but not the skills. Yet the game continued nothing to nothing for three quarters. Randolph was furious. SFU had been in scoring territory four times without making a single point. Coach knew why and that he could do nothing about it.

The line did not consciously let down. Each one of them, however, remembered their star running back's scathing contempt. Try as they might, they could not play up. They were down. The season had been long and arduous. They needed a lift, not criticism, from a team member.

Mike was held out on offense, since Sigurd had regained almost all his agility. Randolph deliberately let the veteran stay in even after Westover's place-kick attempt was blocked for the second time. The clock was running out when Mike approached him at last.

"Coach."

"What is it?" A tight-lipped Randolph was seeing his national ranking evaporate.

"Sigurd's tired."

"You know better than to give me advice."

"Far be it from me," said Mike easily. "But it's first down on their twenty. We need everything we can get. Why not throw in Asher and the big boys for a few plays?"

Randolph stared. "Are you crazy?"

"The pro's do it."

"We're not pro's." Then he said in a low voice, "Look at Danning."

Danning ran off tackle and was smothered by an aroused Ohio State defense.

Randolph called Brown and Tillou to him. They listened and nodded.

Randolph said, "Go in. And Mike . . . you go in, too."

They went onto the field. Dan Kyle blinked, then grinned with excitement. Brown and Tillou went in at the tackles. Mike played the guard alongside Westover. Kyle called the straight-ahead line buck with Danning carrying.

Mike felt the force and inspiration of the Ohio State defenders as he lunged. He took his man astride, then was double teamed by a linebacker. He maintained balance and fought the two of them.

Danning, in a burst of speed and violence, went through a hole, and Asher picked him up in the enemy secondary. Danning never stopped until he was over the goal line.

Westover kicked the point for the game.

In the dressing room Randolph made a speech. "Putting the two big boys in there was Mike Caron's idea. If I hear one more word against our linemen I will take away a uniform. And I don't care what it costs. Read me, all of you. This game was almost lost because of one big mouth." He paused. "Any comment?"

Danning had his head in his locker. Randolph left the room. Danning withdrew his head. His face was flaming. "Big deal. One good block and all is forgotten. You linemen were lousy all afternoon until then."

No use trying to talk to him, Mike thought, though the team would have to be pulled together before the all-important game with the undefeated and untied University of Southern California.

13

"FOOTBALL, IT IS only a game."

"You said that before, Mama," reminded Mike gently. It was eight o'clock of the morning of the game against the University of Southern California. The sun was shining. Mike had not slept the entire night.

"How can you play if you no sleep?" demanded Mama.

"I'm going to try."

She was silent, worrying. The telephone rang and Mike jumped to answer it.

Asher Brown said, "Thought you'd be up, cat."

"I'm an early bird," Mike said.

"On the day of this game who's not? Look, friend, I got a job for you tonight if you want it."

"If I'm able to crawl there, I do."

"It's those people with the little boy. You know, the Cavetts. Bobo's cousins."

"Oh, yeah. The kid who says I'm a hardhead."

Ash chuckled. "There's a kid knows something."

Mike changed the subject. "You want me to pick you up?"

"When you leaving?"

"Would you believe right now?"

"Me and Ambrose, we've been sitting here waiting for the dawn," confessed the Negro end.

"Be right over, friend." Mike hung up. Mama Pia was holding two tickets he had provided. He asked "You sure you don't want to go?"

"Football! Have I not work to do? Is there not enough here without wasting a day in San Fernando Valley?"

"Okay, Mama. But think of me." He kissed her cheek and went out to his car.

She touched the place his lips had brushed and stared at the cardboard slips. When the sound of the auto died away she arranged a shawl over her head and went down to Barney's place.

Barney said, "Mama, you got the ducats?"

"I have decided," she said. "We will go."

"I could get twenty apiece for them," he told her.

"Ducats me no ducats. You sold every week those ducats I gave to you. But now you will escort me to the San Fernando Valley."

"Mike know you're goin'?"

He was talking to Mama Pia's back as she scurried for home, thinking of all the things needing doing. She had not yet worn her Sunday two-piece tweed suit. She knew enough from watching television not to wear a hat, but there was the matter of her hairdo. In the magazines she had learned about hairdos and open-air athletic contests. Mama Pia would not make a fool of herself. She would go to the stadium at least this once fully prepared to see her Mike. Mama Pia shuddered, remembering a scrimmage shot seen on the television. How did they live through it? How would she keep her courage, watching it?

Coach Randolph and Bob Westover greeted the newcomers. "Did you see the pro draft list?"

"Yeah. Danning's name led all the rest."

"Now there'll be no holding him. That's what he wanted. He'll be impossible."

Westover burst forth, "Mike, you should've been on it. If it hadn't been for that accident . . ."

Mike interrupted, "Thanks, pal. But not being on it's the best thing ever happened to me. I don't want to be on it. I know better."

"Asher's on it," said Ambrose happily. "Asher wants to be on it. The Rams want Asher."

The big end said, "Sure, I want it. But I'm not going into business, like Mike."

"Danning better not give us any trouble today," Coach Randolph threatened.

"We've been working all week on that," said Mike. "We've done a lot of talking among ourselves. The line, I mean."

"Both lines," Asher added.

"We have our pride, coach," Mike went on. "Maybe USC can knock us around. But not Danning."

"Yeah," nodded Asher. "And maybe—just maybe—he'll get knocked around if he misbehaves. By me!"

"USC's already rated a touchdown better than us. Talk it up, fellows. Just everybody talk it up."

"Talk won't win ball game, Confucius say," remarked Mike as Dillon called the head coach into the office.

Bob Westover said, "Win, lose or draw, Mike, I'm glad I told you how I feel about that draft."

Mike slapped him hard on the bare shoulder. "I know how you feel, amigo."

Bob looked up from his seat on the bench, one sock in his hand. "Mike, I also wanted to talk to you about our friendship."

"Forget it, pal. It's going to be all right."

"Yes. This week's work—the way it went with the line—cleared things up for us, didn't it?"

"Yes," said Mike. "I didn't know how."

"Neither did I," Bob said. "Or Kathy."

Mike was silent. "I haven't seen Kathy. How is she?"

Bob said, "She didn't want me to tell you."

"Tell me what?"

"She gave the ring back in September."

"She did what?"

"Gave Jimmy Nye back his ring."

Mike said slowly, "In September?"

"After the Michigan game."

"How's Jimmy taking it?" asked Mike.

"He's back with Bobo. You'll be seeing a lot of him today," Bob continued. "Randolph said you'll be seeing action."

"I don't think so. Sigurd's all right. Almost. And Gould's in fine shape."

"Maybe they're all right. But you're starting. You're starting on offense. The way you pulled the team together this week—well, Randolph feels we look to you for reassurance."

"It's you they look to, you're the captain."

"That's different. Coach believes we're both needed in there."

Mike thought a moment, then said slowly, "Last year I wouldn't have liked what I do. Now—I enjoy it. I like being on the suicide squad. I like every minute of it."

Joe Danning whooped in. He was swaggering with confidence.

Mike added, "Almost every minute."

Mama Pia lost her breath on the climb to high seats. She had never been with so many people in one place at one time. She edged past crossed knees, repeating, " 'Scuse, please . . . 'Scuse me, lady . . . 'Scuse me, sir." She came finally to rest, saying, "Doctor Smith, I am here!"

Mike had arranged to seat them together in case

Mama relented at the last moment. Barney had met Smith on previous visits to the stadium. They were bursting with anticipation.

"So many people!" she exclaimed.

"SFU has fifteen thousand students. And they all have friends and relatives. Most are here today. After all, this is going to be the season's big football game." Doctor Smith reeled off facts.

"You think Mike's team wins?" Mama Pia asked anxiously.

"It'll be a tough, hard one."

"Football," she moaned. "Why did I come here?"

"To watch Mike," Barney reminded her.

She leaned close to Doctor Smith. "I must lose my Mike."

"Why, what do you mean, Mama?"

"My Mario is come home next week." She wiped away a tear. "I do not know which way to weep. For joy or for sorrow."

"You should be happy. Now you will have two boys."

"But Mario, he must have back his room."

"Mama, don't cross that bridge 'til you come to it. Be happy. Look, here they come!"

The teams were trotting out of the tunnels. A tremendous roar rose to the clear California sky. Mama arose and cried, "There he is, number forty-nine, my Mike!"

In front of her two middle-aged men smiled in amusement. The larger, a red-haired, red-faced, jug-eared individual, turned and grinned. "Your boy will have his troubles today, lady."

She eyed the fellow. "Trouble he will give, too."

"Caron was a good halfback," said the man. "In the line, he's a greenhorn."

"You will see green! My Mike will . . . pulverize them."

The man's companion laughed and they returned their attention to the field. Mama sat and seethed.

Doctor Smith said, "We win the toss."

"We will receive," she said smartly. She hammered on the red-haired man. "Now you will see, Mister Smart."

"Mama, I thought you knew nothing about football," Doctor Smith said.

"A lady can learn. A lady can look at the television and read the magazines when Mike is gone, can she not?"

The man in front muttered, "I wish you luck, lady."

"My Mike, he is suicide gang," she cried. "He will murder 'em."

"But you hate violence," murmured Doctor Smith, concealing a smile.

"When my Mike hits *them* . . . that is difference!"

USC was ready to kick off. Danning and the slight, quick Brill were back to receive. Everything was hung in the balance. The golden vision of a national championship seared every eye. The whistle sounded shrill and faint and far away.

The ball came up, end over end, drifting down deep into SFU land. Danning rushed in front of Brill and grabbed it, losing the block Brill could have given him. Mike took his appointed man and dumped him hard. When he got up the roar from the crowd was unmistakable. Something offbeat had happened.

He ran back toward the action in time to see Jimmy Nye scoop up the loose ball and scamper over the SFU goal line, laughing in glee. USC had double-teamed Danning, whacked him hard, and made him fumble the ball.

USC kicked the extra point to make it 7 to 0. Mike lined up again, same place, same play. Bob signaled for a different formation. Mike, to protect the runner coming up the middle, was to retreat and pick up the other blockers in a V-type wing.

USC kicked. Brill took it on the goal line. Danning charged to join the flying wedge. He was slapped down by a huge Southern Cal lineman and rolled into the dirt.

Mike picked out Jimmy Nye. As the swift back came down the field, he angled on him. At the last minute Mike slung a blind side block. Nye flew up into the ozone and all the way off the field of action. Mike got up and started for another scarlet jersey. The whistle sounded. Brill was downed on the twenty-five-yard line. Danning's failure had left a breach in the blocker's wall, something no pro scout could miss.

SFU huddled on the fifteen-yard line and Kyle gave

them the signal. They hustled back to the ball on the twenty-five. Mike leaned on one hand, gazing at his opponent. He had digested the contrast between line play on defense and line play on offense. The latter called for instinctive moves, attack, daring. The former called for thoughtful analysis, and the following of patterns clearly depicted in blackboard diagrams. Mike was ready to go.

Foran put one hand on the ball, settled himself. Kyle counted in rhythm. Southern Cal was wary, alert, tense. At the last possible second they began looping, stunting, a maneuver least expected by SFU. The ball went back to Kyle. It had to be Danning's play. To maintain his confidence, he had to be given his chance to atone for his fumble.

Mike and Bob drove ahead, trying to clear out for the SFU running back. Mike felt the brunt of attack. In an instant he knew the truth. The Southern Cals were keying on the big threat . . . Joe Danning.

Bob and Mike could not move the mountain of fighting flesh tossed against them. They had no running room. The play was smothered for a one-yard gain. In the huddle, Danning snarled, "Open it up. If you can't open it up, get outa there and let somebody else in."

Westover snapped, "No talking in the huddle."

Kyle calmly signaled, a fake to Danning, a check-off pass to Manning. Back they went to the line of scrimmage. Again the count, again the snap back.

Mike bowled over his man. The contact felt good. He was ready for Jimmy Nye, went for him on the flank. The whistle blew. Kyle had failed to duck Barnett, the USC linebacker, who slipped through when Pascal pulled out to lead the blockers. Mike expected a blast from the big-mouth running back for the five-yard loss.

It didn't come. They huddled. Danning looked dazed by his own errors, or those of the team. Kyle called his number on third down and they went into action. Danning took the ball. Mike charged, was double-teamed again. Danning got three yards. Kyle went back into his own end zone for the kick.

Ball met instep. Mike peeled off and went down as fast as he could. A tricky USC runner tried to fake him out. Mike dived, grabbed, held on, until Pascal could smother the play on the SFU thirty-seven-yard line.

Mike left but Westover stayed in the game. Ballard played deliberately, running into the line, making three, four yards despite stubborn defense. The USC guards were quick and strong, pulling out or defending their quarterback in the cup. Down-and-outs, and over-the-middle throws found their marks. USC traveled to the ten-yard line.

Randolph called, "Caron!"

"Yes, sir."

"Go in for Gould. They'll be stunting, you know."

Sandy had been playing doggedly but not brilliantly. He had been unable to outthink Ballard, something the middlebacker must do.

Ballard surveyed the situation and set USC in the

famous I formation. Mike jittered into the line, knowing in his heart that Ballard wouldn't dive for the score.

Ballard took the ball. Mike stepped back and clear of the guard's rush. He saw Gallagher, the near-side back, go left while the others went right, and thought, as Ballard rolled out, that it would be a pass.

He moved into the danger zone for a better look. And someone hit him from the blind side. He went down. Ballard ran right over him for the score.

They made it 14 to 0 a moment later. Mike, kicking himself, was amazed that Randolph did not take him out. He lined up for the kickoff, one eye on Jimmy Nye. The ball headed for Brill.

Mike met Nye and rolled with him on the grass. Brill flew past them to SFU's forty-yard line.

Nye growled, "I'll get you yet, you crummy guard, you lineman!"

"Oh, yeah?" Mike saw Sigurd coming in with the other unit for a replacement. "We'll see about that." He trotted off the field. Dillon was waiting for him.

"I blew it," Mike said, "Didn't I?"

"No," said Dillon in flat accents. "They had an extra man in there. They're well coached. We should've had someone with you on the weak side."

"Ballard's smart," Mike said. "They're high."

"And we're not."

Mike said carefully, "We haven't started yet."

"You have. Caron, you're doing good. I want you to know that. You're doing fine."

"Well, thanks."

"Can you get our boys rollin'?"

"They don't love me much."

"Try."

Mike had never thought of himself as a source of inspiration. He was having troubles enough keeping himself under control. But on the bench he sat watching, trying to figure something out, trying to see the flaw in USC's defense.

Kyle was pulling out the stops, trying to shake Danning loose. A USC man was always in the way, keying on Danning every time. Jimmy Nye was all over the place, knocking down Kyle's passes. They exchanged kicks. Mike gradually began to mold a plan that would inspire his teammates.

The quarter drained away. The second period waned with USC content to play a solid game and maintain its lead. Kyle, playing catch-up, put together a couple of first downs with quick passes. But Danning could not shake loose. The two-minute warning was sounded with the ball in USC's possession at midfield, third and five to go.

"Caron, replace Sigurd!"

In the defensive huddle Mike suddenly spoke to Brown. "Asher, I'll be right behind you."

"You suggesting the rush?"

"What have we got to lose?"

"Sixty-five," said Brown.

They all nodded, lighting up a bit. The close-knit defensive unit had been frustrated into playing cautiously. Rushing was a gamble. Brill, back in safety alone, could get snowed under if this failed. Still, the men agreed.

The punter went back, held out his hands. The USC center passed high, forcing the kicker to move to his right to get set to kick.

Asher, with amazing speed for a man his size, hit the blocker protecting the kicker. Mike hurtled past him and into the air. Ball met Mike at chest-level.

Asher, still on his feet, scooped up the pigskin. He made ten yards to the USC thirty before being snagged. Then he got up and ran and hugged Mike, carrying him off the field for all sixty thousand people to see. The television camera panned them to the bench, where Dillon shook hands with them both. "That's better than talkin' it up," the ex pro shouted. "Now, let's see 'em go."

Kyle set them strong right. The clock was running with less than two minutes left in the half. He coolly threw a side lines pass to stop the hands, Danning catching it for five yards.

Then Kyle, as if to pass, faded back on second down. He tried the draw play against the loose USC defense, again handing to Danning. One man put a hand on the halfback's knee. Danning stumbled, lost his balance. The ball popped out of his arms. Manning, following the play, fell on it for no gain. Kyle took time out.

"Caron," came the familiar call from Randolph.

"Yes, sir."

"Go in there."

"Okay, boss." Mike ran onto the field.

They were all breathing hard. Kyle asked if the coach had called a play and Mike told him no. Bob Westover nodded, spoke to his quarterback. "Come right over us."

"For five?"

"For ten," said Bob. "Or more."

"On the thirty-nine, then. Got it?" Kyle asked.

They lined up on the whistle. Mike balanced himself alongside Westover. He looked straight into the USC guard's eyes, promising him trouble. On the count he went forward side by side with Bob. They picked up their men and shoved them. The hole was big enough for the first down.

Danning missed it.

Mike scrambled out from under the pile-up. Danning was already claiming no hole, but his voice was choked, not so loud as usual.

Fourth down and three, and only one play to make. Mike lined up tight, facing his man. Bob went back and Kyle kneeled to place the ball on its point. USC charged but the line held taut. Bob kicked.

Mike watched from beneath three scarlet jerseys. The ball went up and up and on and on. It fell slowly, like a snowflake. The man in the striped shirt threw up his arms.

The score at half was USC 14, SFU 3.

Up in the stands, the jug-eared sport turned. "Lady, your boy can't do it. USC will murder them in the second half."

158

"You see my Mike, what he did? What do you know about it? My Mike, he will show you!"

Doctor Smith said, "Mama, I'm afraid our team is overmatched."

"You, too?" She grew red in the face. "Doctor, you will see, you will see something."

Then she was quiet, eating a hot dog with mustard and drinking coke out of a paper cup, throughout the rest of the period. Her spirit was strong, but subdued. She sat with her hands clasped in her lap, brooding.

In another section, Nancy Waite was saying, "I'm going to have a fainting spell if something doesn't happen."

"Have you been watching Mike closely?" Kathy asked. "Have you seen what he's doing down there?"

"Only when he's close to Bob. I'm dying for Bob."

They sat, worrying.

In the dressing room Mike, for the first time that season, did not retire to his quiet corner. He joined Bob. Randolph was furiously lecturing at the blackboard.

Bob whispered, "Chalk talk won't help."

"You're right," Mike agreed. He spoke directly to Danning. "What do you think?"

"If you guys would open up some holes. . . ." The halfback broke off. His voice was low. "I dunno."

"Look, you blew it. Not us. Remember last year when I blew it?" Mike slapped Danning's arm, hard. "Remember?"

"I remember."

Randolph went into an oration, ended by snapping, "I'm using everyone this half. I'm using Brill at half-back!"

Danning seemed to shrink a little. As if searching for something he stuck his head inside his locker. The team started out, but Mike lingered, motioning for Bob to leave, too.

Mike took Danning's elbow. "Brill can't do it," Mike told him. "He's too light, too small. He's quick but he hasn't got your power. Randolph will be coming back to you."

"You . . . think . . so?"

"Yes. And here's some advice. Forget the pro game. Take it from me, Joe. There's only one corny old bit to remember. We want to win this, all of us. Every single son of us."

He dragged Danning out. USC was to kick off. Mike took his place midfield of the blocking formation. USC kicked deep but Brill, speedy and deceptive, came up from the one-yard line, faking right, then going for the picket fence along the side lines. Mike chose Nye again, banging him head-on, knocking him down. Brill ran over the thirty, then out of bounds, where an over-enthusiastic Southern Cal man piled onto him and received a fifteen-yard penalty for unnecessary roughness.

Brill was white with pain. Danning came running on, lips set, lines deep around his wide mouth.

Nye called nastily to Mike, "You're next for the stretcher."

160

One of his teammates grabbed the defensive back and hauled him roughly into the huddle, scowling. Mike laughed wryly. Kyle set the team strong left from the right-hand marker on the forty-five.

Mike hit his man, then went through, letting the guard make a belated charge. Kyle was throwing to either Danning or Morgan, the wide end. Nye came in, covering Danning. Mike hit him so hard he spun like a top. Kyle threw hard and straight.

Danning got a hand on the ball, ran two steps. The middlebacker hit him hard. The ball bounced into the air in an awkward parabola.

Mike reached for the spinning leather with loving hands. He ran straight ahead for the goal line. Carson and Griffin, the safeties, caught him on the ten-yard line. He dragged them to the five, fighting with all his might for that fat, white goal line. They tumbled him there.

Kyle was grabbing him, hugging him. The huddle formed. Asher Brown and Ambrose came in. Kyle quoted the 39 series. They jumped to position.

Manning had the ball. The USC line rose like a tremendous wave to smother the play, Asher Brown and all. Mike was kicked twice, by accident, in the melee. He got up groggily, staggered a few steps. Sigurd ran in to replace. Mike patted the veteran on the shoulder, said hoarsely, "Take 'em out, pal."

Bob Westover asked anxiously, "How bad is it, roomie?"

Neither noticed the slip of tongue. Mike said, "I'll be back if they want me."

He trotted for the side lines, wrenched off the head-guard, and then heard it.

The stands were chanting, "Ca-ron, Ca-ron, Ca-ron." He lifted his head and grinned. Happiness washed over him. Randolph and Dillon vied with each other and the SFU bench to touch him, pat his shoulder pads, slap him. Trainer Hodges hustled with oxygen, wet towel, and smelling salts. "What down is it?" asked Mike.

"Third and goal," said Hodges. "Them Trojans is tough."

Kyle was deploying the team. Asher and Ambrose loomed large. Mike expected another line plunge with Danning or Bowers. The ball came back. Kyle did not retreat into a cup. He merely backed up two swift steps.

Then he threw a soft, little pass over the heads of the charging Trojans. Morgan caught it over his shoulder in the corner of the end zone. Westover converted. Score: Southern California 14, San Fernando 10. The stands were going crazy.

Bob prepared to kick the ball to USC. Danning sat alone on the bench, wrapped in a blanket although it was not a day for blankets. Slowly, then with decision, Mike approached him.

"Hey, Joe."

"Nice run," Danning said. He looked very unhappy.

"On the thirty-nine series, look for the hole behind Bob and me. Or maybe between us. Play it by ear but keep your head up."

"I won't play again," said Danning. "I know when I'm lousy."

"Sure, you do. You're smarter than I was," said Mike cheerfully. "It took me a long while."

Danning regarded him. "Yeah?"

"Yeah."

"I don't get it."

"Don't try. Just watch us on the thirty-nine series."

Mike moved away without waiting for a reply. Southern Cal had the ball on the thirty. Ballard was calling for inside plays, then a pass, then a draw. The Trojans were superbly coached. Yard by yard they were coming downfield. On the twenty they tried a field goal as Asher and the others held. They missed by a foot.

Still Randolph kept Mike out of the game. The third quarter trickled away without a score by either side. The fourth quarter ground on. Both teams were hitting. The sound could be heard on the side lines, crunch, slam, bang. Everybody was weary but they were up, high, fighting down to the bricks.

Southern California refused to play for time. Ballard kept probing for weakness, looking for breaks, trying for an insurance touchdown to sew it up.

Penalties were imposed as tempers grew short and timing went off. Randolph walked the side lines, muttering to himself, sometimes sending in plays.

The two-minute warning sounded. SFU had the ball deep in its own territory after a fine punt. The coach rapped out, "Caron!"

"Yes, sir."

"Sigurd's had a beating. How do you feel?"

"Fine."

"Go in and . . . just go in there."

Mike adjusted his headpiece and ran onto the field. He reported, whispered to Kyle. "Go with Danning."

"Coach's orders?"

"Nope," said Mike with a touch of his old arrogance. "Mine."

Kyle said, "I see." He called the signal.

They lined up strong left. Mike and Westover timed their move, caught the beat of the call by the quarterback, were a split second quick. They picked up their man and turned him and went on. Danning carried.

Mike hit the linebacker and saw Danning go past him. He made one last dive at Nye, got him midwaist. Danning went to the thirty-yard line.

Mike ran to the huddle. Kyle gave them the 39 series. Manning, back in and fresh, bulled for five.

Kyle had the USC men believing in his running game. He feathered a pass down to Morgan. Another race against time from midfield, first and ten. The passing game wouldn't do now, Mike thought. It was scramble and pray.

Kyle called the draw. Mike faked retreat, then swung out. He was leading the blockers when Nye finally caught him from the side he could not protect. He felt the impact, the pain in his right leg. He went down, hearing Nye laugh.

Danning was held to no gain. Mike closed his jaw and jumped to his feet. He made himself hustle to the huddle. He bent, feeling the pain, but not allowing it to stop him. On the line he held hard against the middle-backer. Kyle again passed to the side lines. Morgan caught it for the first down and a much-needed time-out as he went over the side lines with Nye riding his back.

Ball was on the thirty-nine, now, and the San Fernando fans were whooping it up. The team gathered around Kyle. The quarterback looked at Mike and said, "It's been your day. What's our next move?"

"I'd say hit 'em and hit 'em again." He was resting his leg, trying to keep his voice light. "Joe can do it, all of it."

"You hear him, Joe," said Kyle, keen eyes on the running back.

Danning mumbled something inaudible. Kyle got up with the whistle and gave them the numbers. They hid their weariness. Victory was beckoning. Mike and Bob moved apart, forcing the Trojans to realign. Kyle faked to Manning and gave to Danning. Mike split the opposite way from Bob, trying to take his man out. Nevertheless, Mike's man got a hand on the charging Danning's knee.

The halfback staggered. Mike fell upon his man to break the tackle. Joe spun and ran into another line-backer, seemed to be downed, found balance, spun again. Bob hit the wing. Nye was coming in. Mike got in front of him and rolled. Nye went up into the air. The safeties got Danning on the USC twenty.

One minute to go. Kyle pulled the team in tight and faked to Danning. He rolled out, found the receivers covered. Mike and Bob ran right and Kyle followed. Nye and the safeties rushed. Kyle went out of bounds on the five.

USC wouldn't give. The first plunge was no gain. Danning lost one, Tug Manning came down with his knee on the four. SFU took a precious time-out.

"Fourth and goal," said Bob.

"I wonder what the coach wants?" Kyle asked.

"If he wanted anything, he'd send in a play," Asher Brown said. "He wants us to decide."

"You and Bob decide," Kyle said. His emotions were masked.

Danning was kneeling apart, headguard in hand. Mike looked at him, then at Kyle. Mike said, "I suggest we win the championship."

Bob shrugged. "Dan?"

Kyle said, "I guess it's go for broke." He motioned them all to huddle. "They'll be expecting a pass. How about the split on thirty-nine, Blue and left?"

They marched out with the crowd yelling, settled down in the familiar stance, waited stonily through the long count. The Trojans were not to be drawn off-side. They remained as twenty-two stone men until Danning slowly wheeled and began flanking to the right into a modified double wing, with Ritz flanking left. Kyle snapped his fingers, took the ball from Foran.

Mike and Pascal pulled out like terriers. Mike's leg, despite a flash of flaming pain, did not buckle under him.

Kyle made a quick pitch out to Danning. Bob came

slanting past his man, who trailed the play. The USC linebackers, ends, and wings came flying in. Danning, as if to turn the corner, stretched his legs for the outside. Traffic was far too heavy. The play seemed smothered, the game lost.

Mike and Bob were almost shoulder to shoulder. Mike, without looking back, found voice to roar, "Now, Joe!"

Bob went with him. They turned in and spread apart, each taking a man. Danning, running at top speed, seemed to apply brakes. He dug up turf, threw his hips, came cutting and angling. Mike and Bob went down. Joe skipped between them.

On the one-yard line they grabbed him. Danning took them five yards into the end zone for the touchdown.

Bob converted. Time ran out.

SFU won the big game and the championship of the collegiate world.

Bedlam reigned on the side lines.

Danning came back onto the field. Mike got up slowly, limping. Joe and Bob tried to serve as crutches. Mike shoved them both away, laughing in sheer relief. "Hey, we did it! We got Joe over, didn't we?"

"You sure did," said Joe Danning. "You sure did!"

They barreled into the dressing room. Danning held Mike aside for a moment. "Hey, Mike."

"Yeah, man!"

"A guy can learn a lot in one afternoon, if he gets his skull cracked hard enough."

"You're right, Joe."

Mama Pia's hairdo was no longer neat. The tweed suit was rumpled from jumping up and down and squirming about. She hit the man in front of her one more lick with her purse, saying with a voice grown hoarse from cheering, "Mister, now you see? My boy Mike makes the block. The Trojan horse, he fall down. Joe Danning, he run into the goal and he make the score. Too bad you no understand the football, young fella."

The man stood, grinning from ear to ear. "Lady, I wouldn't go as far as to admit I don't know football. On the other hand, today I was wrong." He stuck out a hand. "My name is Sam Gordon. Glad to have met you, Mrs. Caron."

"I am not Mrs. Caron," she called, but Gordon and friend had moved out of hearing. She turned to Doctor Smith. "A nice man, no? Too bad he don't understand football so very good."

"Mama, Sam Gordon is an ex coach of the Los Angeles Rams of the National Football League."

"So?" Mama smiled happily. "He should know better, then, ha?"

"Er, that's a point. Shall we go down and see Mike?"

"I should tell him now, about Mario. When he is happy. It will be better when we are all happy."

"You're beautiful, Mama," Barney said.

"But I am heartbreak," she sighed. They led her down the steep stadium steps toward the SFU locker room.

14

A TELEVISION CAMERA had been set up to interview the new national champions in the dressing room. Mike found himself called upon to comment. He said very simply, "This has been the greatest season anyone could have experienced. It was a team effort all the way."

By the time he had dressed only Coach Randolph was present. Bob had disappeared. Nancy was waiting for him. Mike understood, he told himself.

Randolph, exhausted, with a big evening ahead, said, "Mike, I'm glad we finally got together. You know how it is with a coach. He has to win. It affects his reasoning, his emotions, everything. But there are meaningful relationships which are, in the end, most important. I think you and I have had one of those."

"Thanks, coach," Mike told him.

They parted on that note. Mike went out into the late sunshine, walked straight into the arms of Mama

Pia. Doctor Smith and Barney were there to shake his hand.

Mama stammered, "Michael, my Michael. I am lose you!" She choked, unable to go on.

Doctor Smith said, "Mario is coming home, Mike."

"How wonderful! Mama, I am so happy for you."

"Me, I am sad. There is no room for my Michael, then."

Doctor Smith spoke diplomatically. "Why don't we talk it over later? Let me take you and Barney to dinner at The Grove, Mama. All the crowd of football people will be there."

"I could not go to dinner in public. No, take me home. Maybe Barney will give us a sandwich?"

"I'll give you the joint!" Barney told her.

Mike saw them to the parking lot, returned for his car. Tonight he had to baby-sit. The Cavetts would be going to The Grove, he imagined. Everyone would be there. Yet somehow he had no desire to be in the midst of that crowd.

He pulled into the driveway of the Cavett house at dusk. He was tired, but his leg hurt only a little. He was thinking about the change to come in his life and about his relationships with Doctor Smith, Coach Randolph, Coach Dillon, the squad, Bob Westover, everyone. It wasn't their fault that he was sad, wistful, lonely. He had brought that upon himself. He carried a textbook to the door and rang the bell.

The Cavetts, ready to depart, were gracious in complimenting him. Mike went in to look at his young friend, who was awake and waiting for him. He said, "Hi."

"Hi, Mike. You won the game."

"Oh, someone told you."

"I listened on the radio. You were the hero."

"There were no heroes."

"Yes, you were. What's it feel like to be a hero?"

Mike thought a moment, smiling at the earnest boy. Then he said, "Maybe it feels good, away down deep. Real good."

"Okay. Then I want to be a hero."

"You're a hero if you go to sleep. Okay?"

"Okay, Mike."

He tucked the boy in, then went slowly into the living room of the comfortable house. It was dark now and he snapped on a lamp. He started for the chair where he usually studied. He stopped, transfixed.

"Kathy?"

She was sitting in the chair. "Hello, Mike. I feel like Mahomet."

"Gee, it's good to see you. What do you mean?"

"Well," she said. "The mountain wouldn't go to Mahomet, so he went to the mountain."

Mike squeezed into the big chair beside her. "Kathy, I'm so sorry for so many things."

She said, "So am I. Most of all for wasted time. I didn't want to waste any more. That's why I asked the Cavetts if I could visit you here."

171

He said, "It's been a long, hard time."

"Very hard. People get mixed up. They don't see things clearly."

"I'm the original mixed-up kid. Or I was," Mike said. "I've been slow to learn." Peace had come to him. He placed his arm around her. "I hope we never part, so long as we live."

"Oh, Mike. I'm so happy. But listen. You're not working tonight. We hired a substitute baby-sitter. Asher fixed it up. He's out in the car."

"And we go to Barney's?"

"No, not to Barney's. To Mama's. To a party."

"Guess who's the happiest guy in town!"

They left the house arm in arm. The substitute baby-sitter, a student, grinning from inside a car parked at the curb, was waiting. Mike gave him strict instructions, then followed Kathy into his car. They drove straight to Mama Pia's.

The house was lighted from porch to back yard. Mama, confused but delighted, met them with outstretched arms. Barney was in the kitchen making pizzas. Doctor Smith was beaming in the background. So were Nancy and Bob. Mama kept babbling in Italian as they all fell to food and strong coffee.

Bob's voice boomed, "Hey, amigo."

"Yeah?" Mike's mouth was full of pizza.

"I hear you're dispossessed."

"Yeah, Mama's tired of me."

Mama screeched to high heaven. Mike got up and went to her and took her in his arms.

172

Bob said, "How about coming back to our place? I'm tired of living alone."

Mike said, "How about that?"

"It's a deal, then?"

"Amigo, it's a deal."

He looked at Mama, so close, at Kathy's shining face, at his friends. He went on, "I'm the luckiest guy in the world. I've got the best people and I've got a goal ahead."

F
REE
REEVE, JOEL
Goal ahead!

5065

DATE DUE			
JAN 2 4 1972			
FEB 3 1972			
OCT 2 5 1972			
NOV 3 0 1972			
OCT 10 73			
OCT 31 '73			
JAN 28 '76			
SEP 2 0 1978			
NOV 2 2 1978			
NOV 5 1985			ALESCO